Zero Day
Blue Jay

Stories

Jeffrey S. Markovitz

LIVINGSTON PRESS
The University of West Alabama

Typesetting and page layout: Kelly West, Joe Taylor
Proofreading: Tricia Taylor, Savannah Beams, Brooke Barger, Kelly West

Cover Design: Kelly West
Cover Art: Eddy Rhenals

Zero Day

Blue Jay

for Amy, Emmie, and Maddie

Contents

Threads

Our mortality is a wound not yet seen.

—Evelyn Emma

When my mother died, I stared at her library for a long time, taking out books at random, leaving gaps of slender knowledge, and refiling them as succinctly as they were first placed. Her bookshelves at oddly inconsistent heights, positioned as precariously as old trees, held fortitudes of knowledge: a lifetime read, dog-eared, margin-noted. Highlighted passages and the passage of her life—perhaps me, a highlight—all that remained of her. I wondered if *she* wondered what would happen to all of her books when she was gone; if someone would select them, inherit them, cherish them as she had—their multi-colored goodness evidenced by the care and wear. Probably, I thought—not cruelly—they would be donated. By me, of course. A thrift store, for poor browsers to find her words by accident, scrawled into the off-white margins left for fresh ink to bond.

It saddened me that I wasn't reader enough to keep them.

But before I could part with them (the only things my left-thinking mother could hoard like a modern-day materialist) I withdrew a particular volume in French I did not know. It was titled *Aucun de nous ne reviendra*, by a woman of whom I had never heard (pictured, presumably it was her, on the cover) but here, amongst the other texts in various languages, she reminded me of my mother. She didn't look like her, but the way she hoisted her chin, a pressed cigarette waiting between two fingers...*that* was my mother. And in the way that moments such as those could succeed to all the moments that would have to be, I realized I would never see her again, and it nearly killed me.

She would have shaken her head at such melodrama.

Flittering through the pages, as I did just to feel their breeze, they stopped on their own accord (as books do when they are so marked) by a small, once-folded piece of paper. It was newsprint, the typical age-yellow of the paper clinging to the pages of the book that held it, like a decades-served prisoner so comforted by his cell that freedom is his only fear. The saved page had two highlighted lines: *Essayez de regarder. Essayez pour voir.* I tried to look for a French-to-English dictionary to see what they meant, but failed, and so pulled the newsprint from the armpit of the spine and unfolded it. It was from 1944 and it was in German. A German text interloping in French print: a 1944 pun at which my mother must have smirked when she placed it. She, of course, being German, could read what was there; I, her shameful American daughter whose childhood was spent pretending away my diversity in sacrifice to the gods of assimilation, knew only a passable bit.

It was a short article, one that didn't even warrant a picture; a deeply buried story about a German war plane that had crashed. I stood there, the book in one hand and the loose sheet of paper in the other, wondering how much the propaganda machine ate holes in the story; truthfully, I was shocked it was even printed. It didn't seem the Reich-way to publicize any—even if small—military defeat; but there it was, black on yellow for the world to see. A crashed German plane. I read crashed, not downed. Apparently, this was a mechanical, rather than an Allied, tumbling.

So there it was: my mother's war relic.

At most, it was a cultural artifact from the war. At least, my mother's eccentricity. But her only daughter, left as I was with a bundle of paper, held it between finger pad and opposing thumb with such force as to pulverize the print into the dust that she was, that we'd all be, that she almost was: then.

She wasn't a survivor; that was the name *they* gave her, afterwards. She was my mother, that fateful, accidental thing between us—a shared body, for a time—that kept us, through death, through abomination, together. But what I was afraid of was that I'd forget her, her face, the way I have my beloved family dog; who I pined for, then cried for, and swore I'd never forget; now just a ripple of audible yawns and the sweet stink of dog breath my fallible memory tried to reconsider. I was afraid I'd forget my mother the same way, the way you wrote a name in sand though the spiteful moon sent waves to melt it away. So I did all I could to collect memories in consideration of nostalgia, worried about a deathbed with nothing to think back on. And the books' pages went *whiff*.

If the walls of the Altenburg factory were invisible, you'd be able to trace the smokestacks down to cauldrons. The spires of industry, announcing civilization from the horizon to distant travelers, led through the roof and down to furnaces that were always angry, and I was the educated woman who kept them growling. Or perhaps not. Perhaps any true utility of mine was just a futile rouse, in the existential sense. Maybe, like everyone, I over-underscored my purpose; maybe I counted too many paces to a place, and forgot all about the steps behind. Maybe, I don't know.

Maybe I was just like the screws that went by.

The factory was an amazing thing. No matter how many days went by, no matter the bizarre looks I received from my comrades, whose eyes were perpetually down, I gazed out. The conveyors that wound along as if dislodged from a tight-wound ball of string, the steam stampers (my name for them), the cauldrons. The walls with no windows. These things, functioning together, taking an inserted material and producing a valuable component: a thing; something useful. Of course I dreaded its use, whatever it was that we were producing at the factory, but I marveled at the ability of construction. The utility of creation. It made me think of motherhood, though I was sure I would never bear a child, no matter how sure I was—that deeply internal holler (like a voice saying, "You will. You will. You will.")—when I was a little girl. I was an older girl then, and as proof that my squandered potential motherhood had suffocated that internal voice, I was rapt by the gears of the production.

Jesus said, "Forgive them Father, for they know not what they do"; and neither did we. We knew not what we created. Gun muzzles tempted their vicious innards inches from our backs, and so we fed the cauldrons, we stamped the steam, we sorted the screws. (This last thing, my job). And I was ironic enough to quote Jesus.

Every day for months (I didn't have the advantage of chalk to hash out, in marks, the days of my imprisonment—how taken for granted they were by my teachers, as they scrawled the chalk to nubs with arithmetic and Latin. I loved, oh how I loved, to read), every day I'd been marched there, the miles to Altenburg, to sort screws on that conveyor. The muzzles behind, buzzing with the audacity of trigger fingers. How audacious the very thought of being human is: such small things with such big designs. And my sorting screws was no more menial than running a country. An army. Than ignoring what was happening in Europe. No, my sorting screws was no more tedious than thinking, even for a second, that being a human is something special.

Some of the screws were as large as my hand (which, wasn't very large) and some were as small as the pads of my fingertips (which, were quite small) and I had to sort them, as they glided by on treads, roller controlled underneath, into bins according to their size.

Every once in a while, I slipped one of the largest into my apron pocket. I believed (I had to believe, with God so elusive, in something) that the largest were the most important. Because I was an animal, because of gravity, I had to believe the biggest things were the most important. Screws. Men.

I never received a tattooed number. That was lore. That was only in some camps. It meant you were a laborer; so what all the following generations would scoff at was a sign of survival to those who bore them. Tattoos meant you were to be counted, and that counting was a subtle, profane indication of life somehow valuable. They were not used in my camp. My forearms were clean of ink, of blood, so I didn't have the reassurance of survival. People must start listening to us and not to history. History has never been honest; it is like blank forearm skin, available for anyone to cut and store ink, while *I* was there. So I know. History is worse when it is filtered through human imagination.

There were too many stereotypes to account for, these so many years later. It was the negative sublime, the thing you stared at and could not describe because it was a palette of colors our brains could not use to paint. It was experiencing the white light of the divine, and pondering why it so seldom shined. Why miracles only happened in the Torah.

How does one beautifully describe emptiness? Silence? These words are near useless.

So many years after the factory, this is what has become of me. A figment, a guest speaker at the endless elementary schools, the endless beautiful young children with their hopeful schoolteachers, asking questions though only half-interested—perked up to not be rude, and I, expected to warm them with a smile, an anecdote, a cheerfully foreign accent. Would it pain them to know the traces of *langue étrangère* they heard in my voice were German? Sometimes the schoolteachers baked yellow-star cookies with *Jude* in black icing on them, which were eaten ravenously by the children.

According the Nuremberg Laws, I was a "Mischling of the first degree," which were, "Persons descendant from two Jewish grandparents but not belonging to the Jewish religion and not married to a Jewish person on Sept. 15, 1935." This bought me time; this and that I inherited the luckier traits of my two *other* grandparents, leaving me all sand-blond hair and sea-blue eyes; that and of course the fact that I'd never stepped foot in a synagogue. But those things only saved me for so long.

Once, back in the Altenburg factory, a comrade saw me put one of the large screws into my apron pocket and exclaimed, "Do not do that; you will be killed."

To which I responded, "I am dead already."

But the muzzle never nuzzled my nape, or my back, or my head. Perhaps they never saw. Or perhaps the soldiers were just as bored as they looked. Most of them were beautiful children with misguided schoolteachers, too. I was efficient enough to sort with my non-dominant hand, so no one seemed to pay much attention to the other hand, buried deep into the pocket, with the screw.

Infrequently but steadily, I snuck my hand into the pocket, which also contained a nail file, and clumsily brushed the abrasive grain (*my father's three-hour beard stubble!*) against the shaft of the screw. Over time—this was all we had: a surplus, a deluge—I learned to file with delicacy, drawing the file back and forth with only the tips of my fingers (second knuckle and above) so that the sinews of my forearm didn't flex or undulate, and give me away. Eventually, I could wear down the threads of the screw's shaft to near nothing, smoothing flat what was designed to grip, before withdrawing the screw, placing it in its bin, and beginning again with another.

When I arrived at the camp near Altenburg from Dresden, they found the file in my pocket (this had been a different pocket; I had been stripped of my previous clothes, made to stand naked long enough to be humiliated, before being given new rags), as they found all of the things in the world that had belonged to me. They took everything but the file. This they let me keep, out of mockery, to laugh at the absurdity that, despite my haggard condition, I could do something as superficial as shape my nails. As my teeth rotted, as my hair thinned, as my muscles betrayed the bone underneath, as my tongue became sandpapered like the blade of the file itself; they'd frequently ask to see my nails—the round clean shape of them, the kept cuticle, the finish of an ocean-loved shell. They'd call to me during marches, "Show us the nails," and I would raise my hands—surrender and spectacle—for them to examine. And their yellowed laughter would seem to catch the sky, echo as if we were all cloistered somewhere. The sound of it triumphant as church bells, psychotic as air-raid sirens, alluring as isle-stayed Sirens, noxious like a snake's kiss. They never worried I'd stab someone: them, myself. The joy of the paradox blunted their boredom and I had fine nails until they began to break. Eventually, they forgot all about it, and so I had the file, and the screws.

I didn't know what good filing the screws would do; I just had to have purpose, some rationality. I had to have something that was mine, just a little agency I could call upon that was geared toward the future. Even if it was a carrot on a string, even if it was so close to nothing that I could laugh at myself for even thinking of it (laughter, even in self-hatred, was balm). It was breath while I was submerged, and so I filed clean the threads of a screw or two a day, no more superficial an action as any other we demand our simple bodies to do. But, of course, the screws had to go to something. We all knew what the bellowing factory was a part of, even if we didn't see the direct result, and it was a human thing for me to do, to hold out hope that my extended toe into the aisle might cause one of them to trip.

I wondered, flightily, as girls did, what people would think and how they would remember all of it. I knew it would end, eventually. How like everything. But posterity—what would it think of this final conclusion: the realization that despite our millennia of egotistical arrogance in thinking we were the champions of the Earth, that we were truly tiered at some class far below the animals. A hundred years hence, when the necessary reality ceded to the eventual mythology, how would the writers appropriate what that was for prose? They would *have to*, of course; the sound waves from our mutable voices would only travel so far; but how would the new voices sound? How would they carry the legacy of this suffering? Could a poem ever be properly impregnated with the dissonant fugue of such rancid melodies? I feared the noblest of future scribes would only be able to get this as a myth, a Trojan Horse, a golden-threaded labyrinth, the words of the Torah flying away from the fire of their own burning pages; but perhaps that is all the past is: a broken circle beyond which the voices of sufferers tremble out into nothing.

A recent evening, I had a nightmare. I was on an interstate, heading from somewhere to somewhere, but there wasn't a single exit offering reprieve from the infinite stretch. All that existed was flat road—long grey expanse bisected by yellow paint and flanked by high concrete dividers. No shoulder, no green signs marking the impending escape routes. It moved on forever, road to horizon like the prize-winning photographs of the American desert, but I was horrified. The interstate in its grandiosity, linking one side of the country to the other, zagging like a heartbeat blip across the landscape: north/south plummets and hikes with marginal east/west progress. My rational mind would know that ocean was inevitable, but my dreaming mind interpreted the web as suburban murder. It was all going and no stopping, all destination and no journey. How horrible it was to go on forever and never get off. How horrible to see all the things one could experience just beyond the shoulders, but be caught in a racing thing only interested in forward so that all those roadside attractions became blurs of the stuff memory lusts for, but like in dreams, were gone the more one tried to remember them after waking. It was because of words; it was because we tried to use words to describe dreams, and they were not the things of words. They were beyond words. Dreams and nightmares both.

I remember when my mother first told me of the screws.

We were on a trip to Philadelphia, a city she loved; it was the first place she lived in America and I always thought this brought her some kind of affection for a place I thought was rather dirty. She wanted to walk me around her old neighborhood, which she painstakingly plotted out on maps but had trouble, on the ground, locating. We wandered, presuming which direction to go (her head shaking negative at how quickly, how much, things changed) until we eventually just decided that where we were was in fact the neighborhood in which she once lived. It was a simple self-deception, the ruse of it just a platform of nostalgia; but for her, it worked. She gleamed with pride at the concrete of the sidewalks upon which she may or may not have ever walked. I was less astonished, the evidence of this in my face or in the small action of my kicking away a piece of trash rather than stepping over it. To all of this, she replied, "What is the greater talent, loving Paris? A place everyone knows to love? Or loving Philly, a place you have to work to love? Isn't there a greater talent in loving something that isn't so obvious? Expectations are really just a matter of consensus."

"Beauty is Truth," I said, quoting a literature class in which I was then in the throes. I was a college student then, and pretension was no less an exercise of common course than waking and breathing.

"Beauty is no such thing," she said, becoming serious.

"Truth—whose truth? Beauty is most in what is false, what *isn't* obvious."

She told me about the filing of the screw threads in a café toward the center of the city, where we sat as two women with drinks and a shared cheese danish. She explained the nail file, the clandestine wearing-away of a screw-or-two-a-day in opposition of some phantasm. She told that story with a sense of pride that I could not understand; I could not see the heroism, the valiance she purported to own in this small act of courage. I was, generally—as most people were and should have been— in awe of my mother and what she had been through. Embarrassed as a small child—at the attention she got, at her fame—the feeling ceded to admiration as my high school then college classes matured me to understand what all of it was and what it meant for her to have survived. But my precocious-if-arrogant collegiate mind, there in that café in Philadelphia, for whatever reason, found the screw filing to be an act of futility so mind-numbing that I could not help the slight tone of condescension that entered my voice.

"What I really want to know, Mom, is why people didn't *really* resist. You know? I mean, they were outnumbered, right? I mean, how could you just let that happen to you? Take it like it was okay?" This was the most defeated she'd ever looked at me. She, so manhandled by life, could do nothing but muster disappointment in her only daughter. And so she responded by saying nothing.

It occurred to me, just like in my dream: no words.

Essayez de regarder. Essayez pour voir.

In front of her bookshelves, the page her newspaper clipping marked remained open in my hands and I realized I had been standing there for an unknowable amount of time. I had conjured this memory of her, in the café, suddenly, without spur. But as I looked back to the yellowed dryness of the newspaper clipping, it suddenly occurred to me that the memory was not, in fact, conjured from nothing. It was there in the article. Perhaps my passing German had neglected it, or perhaps I wanted to unconsciously fail at realizing it, but there it was, seemingly the boldest word in the paragraph. The crashed German war plane. Just after taking off from the Altenburg airstrip. A faulty *schraube*.

And Philadelphia was beautiful.

And I looked up at her bookshelves, wondering what other impossible stories of false beauty—the best kind—lived in the pages there.

At the shoreline I write my mother's name in the sand.

The ocean comes, incessant as history, sacred as the whole world, and tries to erase her. I stand between her name and the water, guarding it with my feet.

Like the words of the Torah, the letters fly.

—for Olivia

for J.U. and J.D.S.

Jerome Colbourne hadn't published a collection of poetry in sixty years, and when he died, he left his wife everything. Which was nothing.

Eleanor Colbourne shuffled the pages of his final manuscript, feeling the slight wind from their whipping, the scent of her husband in that wind, his molecules fluttering from the words on the pages he wrote. He was gone, but as she read the poems, at random, she could invoke him. Him. Unmistakably him, even in the molecules of skin from his fingers.

He had titled the collection *Blue Jay's Last Day*; fitting, Eleanor thought, for him to arrive at the title after working so long on the poems only to die before he could give them away. Jerome would think himself a blue jay, she thought, beautiful to look at, awful to listen to. You get a few in your yard and at first feel like the luckiest girl alive; then they speak.

But when Jerome spoke, the masses heard bells.

His first two collections of poetry were published before he was twenty-five. The *New York Times* likened him to Keats in his youthful ardor and poetic mythological knowledge, adding, "The world collectively holds its breath for Colbourne's injected TB test to stay flat, so that he may never visit Rome's Spanish Steps and so keep us in the color of his flight." He was awarded a seat in an English Department, spent summers lecturing abroad about Americana and the poetic tradition, and married Eleanor.

They had met before he'd written a word, and it was this that confirmed his desired commitment to her; she did not understand him as a poet, an artist, or any such mystical orator. She knew him as the humble man who ate heavily but wished he didn't, read by candlelight only, and turned from her after making love to sigh into the cold side of his pillow. Eleanor was the BC era of his AD poetic career, and because she was willing to be taken, he took.

With his mighty renown and economic stability, they retired to a small unpretentious row home on Delancey Street, which happened to be one of the most pretentious addresses in Philadelphia. They paid too much for the tiny home, but it—and the cobbles—reminded Jerome of Europe, and the attic's pitched roof room, with single window like a vigilant oculus to the street below, was the perfect environment for him to write his third collection of poetry. When it was published, Jerome had just turned thirty. Eleanor did not remember which awards it had been short-listed for, which awards it had won, which speech he'd given in recognition of receiving the key to which city; all she knew was that, after a year of the galore that was Jerome's mad ascent into the canon, after his knighting as a man of letters, he stopped.

In his hamlet of an attic study, Eleanor read some of the poems again at random. They were, she knew, good. "Good." That was the word she knew to use (*she* was never the word-smith). They were more than good, more than great, more than any superlative she could attribute to an achievement. What she knew most of all: they were the best poems he'd ever written. A collection, sixty years in production, finished just before his ninetieth birthday (his last) and enough to secure his stature as one of America's finest scribes. Perhaps even a bronze statue with wizened eyes on his university's campus would be called for.

But for Eleanor, of far more immediate importance was what the publishers would offer for the manuscript. Having never played the agent game, Jerome represented himself; and now, at his demise, Eleanor began fielding a mighty number of calls (mostly before what could be considered appropriate) to her personal residence (alas, now only hers) from publishers about potential posthumous publications. So antagonistic to them in life with his reticence and non-prolificness, they saw Jerome's death as a blessing; if they couldn't get at his mind while he was alive, an autopsy (poetically) was sure to harvest for them the gold they'd been frothing for for decades. The house on Delancey had been paid for, but there was still property tax; there was the desire to leave a financial legacy to her children and grandchildren—and all the money from years of royalties was gone.

Jerome was a good man by many standards, but he was also a man by many good standards. He had his vices. He gambled, not at the table as much as with investing. It amazed Eleanor how a man so literary, so whatever side of the brain it was that regulated creativity over science and economics (Jerome hated numbers so much he argued endlessly—ultimately futilely—with a publisher about excluding pagination from his books, said it ordered the spontaneity of his poetry), so worldly in his travels and his reading—how a man like that would put so much of his money into systems of investment he never understood. She rationalized it as part and parcel with living in a capitalistic country, a place where no matter one's net worth, one was never completely worthy. Not really ever. Jerome got a lot of advice from investment managers. He trusted advising; it was part of his job as a professor. He trusted the advice he gave to students in the comfortable small office at the university he regarded as a second home, designed similarly to the attic study on Delancey. He believed in how he guided them. And so he believed in how he was guided, all of his ducks in a row, quacking in the legs of the V, behind a leader accidentally flying north for the winter.

They had lost everything the year before his death, which prompted Jerome to finally break his sixty-year poetic silence and publish another volume. Outside of these gambles, Jerome's only other stumble was his affair.

Eleanor never knew what made him stop publishing. That is to say, he never stopped writing; only, he never again let anyone read his poems. Not publishers, not magazines, not students, not Eleanor. He wrote, feverishly as ever, editing relentlessly in his attic, wrote through the painful years when the affair became apparent to Eleanor, and they had the duel over the negotiations that would either save or drown their marriage; worked through his lamentations and recapitulations, through his promise that it was over, through the eventual truth that it was.

He wrote on. On until he was eighty-nine, broke, and until a new work, a life's work, would be the only thing that reclaimed any semblance of an estate for him and his. By then, *Blue Jay* was Bible-thick even with pages Bible-thin. It is not fair to say he loved the book, no writer truly ever can, but he considered it complete. Then he died.

Eleanor didn't know why he stopped publishing and never asked. She believed it to be some eccentric artist's protest of the system or something of the kind. She didn't have the nerve to ruminate on the delicacies of a poetic mind; the mind she cared for was housed in a man that, for her, was the poem himself. Jerome had been correct: her investment in him, the poet, was less than her investment in him, the man.

In Eleanor's hands was the only copy of the new collection, typed from his old typewriter. She read on, randomly; the pages weren't paginated. Inside were the words of her husband, unblemished, man-made language; words so tenderly Jerome that she held them to her eyes, then held the pages to her chest. It was years since the affair, and Jerome's subsequent fidelity resounded cavernously louder than it ever had. The succeeding years had been comfort; their little home, puppies to dogs to bones to new puppies. She was an old woman now, and her husband had given a double gift. To her, it was financial liberation. To the world, his words again.

Satisfied to whatever extent a woman can be who has lost her husband but has found a relic of him, she placed the manuscript back onto Jerome's desk. *Blue Jay's Last Day*; indeed, and perhaps its song wouldn't be crooked. It meant so much to her, so much to the world. As she turned to leave the attic, a thin draft from the window cut into the room and lifted the title page from the manuscript, depositing it on the floor at Eleanor's feet. *Last Day*. She picked it up to return it to its others, and in doing so, saw the second page, a page she'd missed in her random reading.

She placed the manuscript in the metal wastebasket by the desk in his old attic and cracked the window. It was on that desk the poems had been born: a nursery, an orphanage. It was there that he spent his time away from her, rapt in desperate attention to craft and detail, in sonorous incantation, in unobstructed diffidence to the street below or world beyond. Upon that chair, in front of that small window, her husband sat with his poems in his arms, tender lover—Eleanor waiting always downstairs. When the flame from her match touched the corner of the top page, the manuscript caught immediately, as if it wanted effigy. Or perhaps it was Jerome's molecules, his skin gasoline, his fingers rogue parents thirsty for infanticide, that fueled the burn. Regardless, they were gone quickly; Eleanor was surprised at how much smoke they caused. The last words caught in the pyre, just beyond the title page, a dedication: —*for Olivia*. Then they, too, went, bones.

Harold and Madeline

I

Their house sat white against the sun at the end of a spiraling road that wound around a hill, carving asphalt into green tree-dense West Virginia. The white was a paint applied by Harold sixty years previously (originally) and touched-up about every five ever since— applied to the old wood siding that he'd fixed upon the wooden skeleton of the house he'd built on that hill. Twelve coats of paint that if carbon-dated, if peeled away and examined, could reveal the age of the house like a bisection of rings in an ancient tree. From the porch, he could see the town, the small mountain town in the small mountain state, segregated by a swath of river, mended with bridges, and busy with the sub-metropolitan ambling of slow pick-up trucks and scuttling denizens.

Now, at ninety, Harold sat over the town, upon the porch he could no longer paint, holding a mandolin with no strings, and humming the tune to a song he'd sung to his great-grandchildren, sporadically allowing lyrics to intercede with the strumming of his throat.

But the cat came back
The very next day.
The cat came back,
I thought he was a goner
But the cat came back,
He just wouldn't stay away.

The great-grandchildren lived states away, and no longer heard the crooning of the old throat.

II

It was Madeline who had the skin, the sort that seemed too bright in black-and-white photos from the time when photos were a novelty. With film and single-flash bulbs flaring kamikaze-suicide into nothing, each shot was everything. Like wedding rings. And Madeline had the skin; black-and-white red-darkroom developed skin that looked decked in powder, puffing out beyond the dark lines that divided her face from the background of the photograph; ethereal skin diffusing beyond the face, held in place only by the imaginations of rapt gazers who knew that skin belonged stuck fast to bones.

Harold treasured this photograph of Madeline, mostly because, like wedding rings, he got his everything-shot, and her skin wasn't chemicals stealing images from life. She was real, in his handmade home, his only wife.

On storm days, perhaps in October when the Earth tried to retain summer heat, holding warmth against the impending autumn so that vicious storms turned a sunset into a threatening grey-pink of cloud cover—unnatural filters to view the wounding world—on days like that, Harold and Madeline stared from their porch, a wooden door squeaky in its oscillation, an old dog with its head between its paws in concern. Even into old age, having buried both of their children (and that old dog), they enjoyed that view from the porch, the impending wrath of storm, that distant metaphor for the trials of life, their proximity a furlough from living's disaster.

He'd hold her around the shoulders until the first of the rain, like that, until the day she died.

III

The last time Harold saw his son alive he hugged him, a man no greater than any man, and thought to himself *this is the last I will see my son alive*. When news came that his premonition had been correct, he flew down to Florida to collect his son's body and things. An old suitcase with his son's initials: in it the contents of a sporadic life, cut from nomadic cloth and tempered—indeed upon anvils—by an alcoholism wrought from Caribbean leaves of absence from the Navy and permanent stays from the military boredom of after-war. In addition, a poorly-tuned mandolin. *The dexterity of those fingers*, he thought.

He reserved a seat for himself and a storage cabin for his son, and rode the long way upon iron rails back home; the casket in a car behind, Harold feeling like he was pulling his son with inertia: the world stopped, the body tumbling along. He thought of what to say to

Madeline, what to say when bringing a body home that came from her body. As if he could say, remember this? This came from you. I return it. Decayed, gone, like a winter plant. This is life and we're meant to see only a third of it, but here we are, seeing all of it. What is there to do?

He had known ever since that hug. Sometimes, the world gives those feelings, those throes of separation where one human spirit, once so entrenched in another, is lifted and brought away, so the sad nostalgia can begin where the reserved understanding that every relationship (even with Madeline, surely) would end—that feeling can settle in for good.

All along the train ride back to West Virginia he tried tuning the mandolin, his fingers inept and the science of music lost on him, until one-by-one, the tuning knob straining under the winding, each string broke.

IV

The small-town post-office was built at the apex of the main street and met the sidewalk with a regal façade: the faux neo-Greco alabaster plaster columns married American red brickwork beyond the entrance doors and achieved only a moment of prestige before admitting the town's mail recipients to the finger-grease rubbed rows of PO boxes and sloth lines of packages tenderly supported by human hands toward counters of incalculable travel. There, Harold, in his amplest of years, would go—after his four a.m. coffee at the twenty-four hour diner ("Mornin', Rose." "Mornin', Harold.")—straight past the line of waiting customers to the counter to flirt with young Harriet, all but twenty, who humored the old man with innocuous toleration in the safety of useless and involatile muscles: slow, living atrophy.

"Oh, Harriet."

"Oh, Harold."

"I'm gonna take *you* ta dinner."

"Oh yeah, Harold? That's what you always say. When?"

"One of these days."

"I'll believe that when I see it."

Then she'd turn to the nearest customer and remark, "He's been comin' in here ever'day for clear over a year and sayin' that he'd take me to dinner, and you know what?, empty promises."

"I will though," he'd say to the customer, the flirtation carrying through sometimes bemused and other times impatient listeners who, in small-town fashion, also tolerated the aged enough to politely listen.

"He's sweet on me," Harriet would say.

Then one late afternoon, when she got off work, Harold was there by the back door in a tolerably good suit with matching brown fedora. He crooked his arm and she took it, and for the second time that day, he opened the door of the twenty-four hour diner.

V

When Archie was born, Madeline was relieved that her body wasn't broken. That's all she thought, throughout labor, throughout the pains of his entrance: that what she was hearing, the tearing of her body, was the breaking of it; that it would never return to normal. She was all but twenty, a new mother, this new thing that had such alarming connotation.

Harold stood proudly beyond her outstretched legs. In his arms was a white towel conformed to a writhing thing, and what she focused on was the bloody hand print on the towel from Harold's hand's caressing the shape of her son.

He brought Archie (not yet Archie) over to her and laid him on her chest and she said, "Archie" and he replied, "Archie" and their son was then Archie.

There was a strangeness in the addition to the family. It was as if their unit could finally be called a family. In the marital joy that was their union in the first years of marriage (unlike so many of their contemporaries, Harold and Madeline waited a few years to have children) they thought of themselves as a lucky couple: just two people who shared a devotion to one found person improbable in the millions of people one could find in the world. When Archie came, it appeared to them that they had matriculated into something else; they were responsible for the creation of life, and in that redundant human feat they had become more than a couple; they were a family. It was a decisive and exact and perfect thing. So they did it again, this time Madeline saying, "Kate" and Harold replying, "Kate" and Archie's sister was then Kate.

VI

Harold says Archie invented BQ5 Sonar while in the Navy.

Harold says Archie was a SEAL.

Harold says Archie's bunk in the submarine gave him permanent claustrophobia.

Harold says the sailors took leave in St. Thomas.

Harold says on St. Thomas was the goddamn rum.

Harold still doubts if Thomas should have been canonized at all.

VII

Madeline fried bacon in a cast-iron skillet, one that she didn't clean with water, just wiped with a cloth and let dry so that every meal she cooked in it retained a bit of the previous meal's flavor—a collection of dinners with traces of one another throughout the endless years that do nothing to iron but did everything to her. She never drained the skillet of the grease that bled from the bacon strips while cooking. She didn't use plastic shrink-wrapped store-bought bacon, but pork bacon cut from the hides of recent-dead pigs from local farmers; this sort of bacon bled extra sweet grease. She left it in the skillet, using it as a simmering pool for the next round. She cooked endless strips of bacon on Sundays. Harold, Archie, and Kate ate plenty, ringed around an old wood table, the legs inch-crooked gapped among one another, paint all but chipped away. The radio played staticky songs from its fabric mouth, puffing it out in a pout.

When the once-pig had become blackened porcine strips, married to the most irresistible smell on Earth, Madeline would leave the skillet and its grease to congeal. For lunch, she'd scrape layers of the soap-white lard from the skillet and spread it on to toast. They all ate.

VIII

There wasn't a day at the old nursing home that Harold didn't visit Madeline. Her stroke had left her in a placid supine state, permanent to her back when not rolled to circumvent bed sores. But she could moan, and did so mostly in Harold's presence. So when he was too weak to roll her, distant relations—their suggestion—helped him admit her to a home—to wait—where he would abuse the epithet "visiting hours" each day, on rounds from the diner and back home. In the metaphysical musing and longing of the mind, Harold interpreted Madeline's moans, translated them, from the indecipherable to his name; he came half because he needed her and half because her moans were her needing him. Calling.

When she passed she did so with the coolness of end-life padded by the stillness and old-scent of nursing homes, a sort of eyes shutting that should have been so much more. All those years and no sort of expressive end; just one look over then eyes gliding—as if to sleep—down, but not to sleep. Harold supposed he was as proud of that as anything. Just shut your eyes, dear. She'd not want to make a fuss. He was proud of her, like that, just at the end.

When she was in Earth, next to son, he took the opportunity to accompany a distant relative, a truck driver, as cab companion in a shipping voyage across France. He hadn't been to Europe since the war, and he rode mostly silently, watching the French countryside cede to French towns then reappear as the people and buildings dissipated into the peculiar yellow of it all.

IX

Madeline bit her nails through the war, bit them when Harold wrote. She feared the words he wrote on the envelopes of letters: her name and his own home, in a shaking scrawl that shook worse with the weeks—she feared them more than government issued, short-lined death decrees, because she feared she'd be reading the unsettling of his strong mind, wrestled from him in the form of blood and ripping (Earth, borders, bodies). But his letters were always jovial, jests and romantic quips of Europe, of missing West Virginia, of her hair.

Adel—

Poland flat. God steam-rolled, laid sod. Pretty hard up for a roll of hill around here. Most guys whining about food, I think they just cook things too short. It's the char they want, right? They say there's a war going on around here but I just see the same old humanity, nit-picking and pinching and running away like always. Don't believe everything you read; I'm on vacation. Will have a cup of cap in Milan before I come home, so don't moan for me, Tiny.

Love to Archie, love to Kate.

—Har

and

Maddy—

> *Damnedest thing. There we are walking the fields—you should see the endlessness of the fields; it's like the whole damn continent is uninhabited save for dry produce. Everything almost yellow. But there we are, field walking, and we hit what they're calling a camp. Well, I won't bore you a bit about it, but I'll say it's a shame what folks do when pressed (or not). Sometimes I try to figure what kind of species we are, anyway. Mutts seem better, times (how's ours?). But all that's morose. Strange, main thing was it made me think of you all again. Stronger, though, this time. I sort of just began to feel appreciative. Funny, huh, appreciative all these miles away. But appreciative still. Don't know why, miss your hair. And don't go around flaunting it when I get home and I complain about you arguing to always get what you want. It's the heat of the moment, Mads, remember that. Don't whip this old leaf out when I won't move the couch or pull out a jutting nail, or something.*

> *Love to Archie, love to Kate.*

> *—Har*

X

Madeline let her great-grandchildren use the old label maker, a big, wheeled device with trigger that spewed long scrolling type-writer fonted strips—adhesive backed—that she and Harold hadn't used for years. It once served the purpose to remind the men of the house where things were (and were supposed to be), but for many years had sat in an armoire behind glass doors, the glue under the protective paper backing the plastic strips either holding to its stickiness or drying to nothing.

Now, her great-grandchildren, who lived states away, two boys, made countless strips of their names and other childish sayings, sticking them to surfaces: tables, walls—pulling the trigger of the machine until the mechanism inside cut the label from the unblemished coil within.

> Ralphie was here.
> So was Danny.

Madeline didn't care about the announcement of these people, in plastic strip form, all over her house. Their names, push-stamped from the machine, resounding from her walls (only so far up), from the floor, in the mysterious places only children can go. They were Archie's daughter's children, and Archie had been gone for some time. Their movements reminded her of him, his almost-lankiness, Ralphie's big build, Danny's precocious head cock; they could do whatever they wanted in the week-a-year they spent in Harold's and her home. When they'd go, she wouldn't remove the labels; they'd fall on their own accord, that old glue only so strong.

"Sing the old song, Papu," they'd call to Harold. And so he did. And they'd transcribe it in label, stick it to the wall.

> The cat came back.
> He just wouldn't stay away.

XI

The alliance of blood is a tremendous and preposterous thing. It calls people through miles. It leans upon the familial as if a person were a cane; it is always geriatric, the alliance, and needs needs needs. It is an elastic cord, straining the most at the greatest distance, rejecting turn-aways, hating footsteps Doppler-elongating thumps away. It stays with a person, throughout their life, like a guilt, a thousand should-haves; parents caring for children so they can be cared for in their old age, children booking flights across the too-big country (that's not big enough) for long-weekend visits to grandparents—quota—half looking forward to their death (because gravestones are easier [sadder, but easier] to visit) and half hating that the thought crossed their minds.

But, as for the tremendous: how, in the world, there are other people who, regardless of anything, do and will always, love you.

XII

The way they bury a Navy man is by firing seven rifles three

29

times, uncovering the casket of its draped American flag, folding it into a tight triangle, and presenting it to family.

They gave Archie's flag to his daughter. She, twenty-four; her own son, there, unaware, three. He was born when she owned as many years as the fictional bullets that rifled into the sky at her father's burial. She had long moved states away.

Harold held her one shaking forearm; her hands were stuck-fast to the cloth triangle braced against her chest. Madeline sat behind her, looking at nothing but the back of her neck. Nape. There was a mole there, small, skin level, bereft of any serious topography, bereft of any serious threat. But this was the small button Madeline watched quiver, watched heave with uncontrol, watched settle for minutes. This was Madeline's granddaughter, a flower from her flower, ripe-alive, and next to her, her great-grandson, another part of the botany. From left to right: Harold—Their Granddaughter—Their Great-Grandson: a genus in garden sequence. Flowers reproducing. She saw suddenly, as they lowered her son into the Earth, as a trumpet tapped, how humans beget humans and that was it, and the perfection of it.

The nape mole that she couldn't help but love with reckless uncontrol.

XIII

When Harold and Madeline celebrated their first anniversary, they went to a park near their home that overlooked their town, and waited with a camera on a small green park bench. When a passerby passed by, Harold momentarily arrested them, explained it was their anniversary, and asked if the person would take their photo. Obliging, the person took the photo as Madeline held up one finger.

When Harold and Madeline celebrated their second anniversary, they went to a park near their home that overlooked their town, and waited with a camera on a small green park bench. When a passerby passed by, Harold momentarily arrested them, explained it was their anniversary, and asked if the person would take their photo. Obliging, the person took the photo as Madeline held up two fingers.

When Harold and Madeline celebrated their third anniversary, they went to a park near their home that overlooked their town, and waited with a camera on a small green park bench. When a passerby passed by, Harold momentarily arrested them, explained it was their anniversary, and asked if the person would take their photo. Obliging, the person took the photo as Madeline held up three fingers.

On their bookshelf, they had an album where each page featured the aging couple, over decades, the only thing changing was the amount of fingers they held up in the succeeding photos.

XIV

On their modest bookshelf, made from strong wood but supporting only scant literature, rested random tomes from a passing collection of words collected over the course of a life and in the form of borrowings, occasional yard-sale pick-ups, and whimsical bookstore purchases. Neither Harold nor Madeline read often; it was Kate who, after enrolling at West Virginia University, would come home with anthologies of literature and rhetoric, polemics on social justice, foreign language textbooks; and deposit them for safe-keeping on the old shelves of her parents' house. Over the course of her first two years, Kate had dentured a bookshelf of previously missing teeth with new and intellectual texts, enough to make a visitor prop up their eloquence in the company of such adept literates.

A few years later, Kate would remove those additions from the bookshelf when she relocated to her own home, freshly graduated, freshly married, freshly invigorated by a world that opened—no, not like a book—like a prairie in front of her, all sky and horizon sewn with perfect seam, a caesura at such an impossible distance that it seemed to her nothing could distract from the potential of existence.

Left amongst Harold and Madeline's books was a collection of poetry Harold had brought home from the war. After Germany, he briefly visited Spain, purchased the book of poems written completely in Spanish (a language he did not speak) and brought it home to West Virginia. After Kate left, Madeline dusted the bookshelf (an unnecessary act as the books that acted as previous residents took their own dust with them) and came across Harold's war relic book. *El Peso del Beso*.

She brought it to him, sitting with a coffee, out on the porch, and asked, for the first time in all those years, what it meant. He got up, went to her, and kissed her hard.

XV

West Virginia reached with its arm outstretched, as if trying to jut into neighboring states. Its northern sprawling arm seemed to stretch to separate the jilting lovers of Pennsylvania and Ohio; or perhaps it reached for the Great Lake. It was mostly wild-land; hills: almost mountains, rivers: sometimes rapids, trees: clustered and dominant; the interstate slicing across its chest like a pageant sash. Mostly it was slow. Even when Harold was ninety, there were roads that had not been paved, miles between neighbors, outhouses. It was not as if West Virginia was nostalgic about the past or inept at the present (or, additionally, disinterested in the future); it was more as if it found contentment in a time and simply stuck to it. As if, along the course of human progress, a moment came when the state itself thought, indeed, this is how it will be, and decided then and there to allow the rest of the world to move forward on a timeline while it remained present on a hash mark.

Its wilderness synced with that moment, its wildness linked forever and intrinsically with a pretty allowance of everything else to move away from what it most loved: a singular moment.

Its people felt like this too.

XVI

When the chemotherapy finally did its best by doing its worst, Kate threw up her hands and said, "This is it." She and her husband took leaves of absences from their jobs and drove across the United States with their five-year-old Labrador and a camping tent. They stayed in National Parks, backwoods, and on the reclined seats of their small car in rest-stop parking lots. They made love, made fajitas in tin foil over open flames, and photographed the grandiosity of the still-mystical and wonderful country. She was just over forty. At Archie's funeral, she stared at the hole that would consume him, and thought of cremation.

At the Badlands, she explained to her husband how being a professor at a university created a strange timeline in a person's soul. Years floated on in clumps of two semesters, so unlike the common forty-hour workweek. To split a year in two fifteen-week blocks caused a strange segregation in life: it sped it and slowed it down simultaneously. Sped it because new academic years, so quick to come, meant a calendar year had elapsed. Slowed it down because of the tranquil times between lectures in office hours, time that her husband half-chidingly claimed she wasn't working at all, but of course, as all teachers know, she was.

At the Great Sand Dunes of Colorado she recalled her childhood with Harold and Madeline. They too had taken her to walk enormous mounds of sand in high temperatures; but she couldn't remember where.

And at Glacier, they hiked to the Grinnell Glacier Overlook, a taxing journey that their Labrador could not complete, so they left him at the midpoint chalet, borrowed jackets there, and went on. A grizzly bear burrowed only yards from where they hiked, but they made the summit. There, Kate told her husband that she was afraid.

And at Yosemite, lying to sleep in the open air under the wilderness, Kate said, "The wind in the leaves sounds like rain."

She was cremated.

XVII

"Archie, I wanna tell you somethin'."

"Yeah, Pa?"

"You see how that fire moves? How it wraps itself round the wood and also eats through it? You see how it whips up and disappears when its stretches too far?"

"Yeah, I see it, Pa."

"That's because fire is alive. I want you to remember that, Archie. When we come up here to camp like we do, or when you camp with your children one day, or whatever, remember that fire is alive."

"Fire is alive."

"That's right. And I don't mean this campfire only, neither. All of it. A candle's flame, a forest fire, same. And when you snuff it, you snuff a life. Candle flame might last a few minutes is all. Match strike, a couple seconds. Forest fire, a few days. But they live and they die and there's no tragedy in any of it, Archie. Just remember the way it dances, and how much it loves the wood it eats. That's about all there is to anything. Can you remember that, Archie, no matter what?"

"Sure thing, Pa."

"That's good. No one gets to miss the burn. Now how about I fix you a s'more? Hand me a mallow. That's right; now, how do you want it."

"Scorched."

"I know that's how you like it."

"I know you know, Pa."

XVIII

"And she's mine," Harold said to Ralphie, pointing down to the grass that would be displaced only to place him inside. It was a plot next to Madeline, and at first Ralphie thought his great-grandfather was talking about his deceased wife, but then realized he had used the feminized pronoun to describe the hole that was not there but would be.

The two had made the short trip to the cemetery on the first trip Ralphie had come to visit Harold on his own. He was in graduate school in Pittsburgh, and drove the short distance to slow West Virginia to see his great-grandfather and to note where his relations were buried. While Harold drove them to the cemetery, Ralphie copied directions into a notebook.

"And that's Archie, your grandpa."

"I remember the funeral, Papu."

"Do you? Why, you was just a little un back then."

"I remember the rifles."

"Scared you, I reckon. Strange, how many years ago that was. One thing I've learned, Ralphie, is that no matter how many years go by, it still never seems like that long ago."

"What doesn't?"

"Well, anything, I guess. Nothin' seems that long ago."

"Where's great-aunt Kate?"

"Scattered. Ashes."

"Cremated."

"Yeah."

"But not you," Ralphie said, smiling, slapping Harold gently on the forearm. "You're for her."

"That I am, Ralphie."

The two stood there over their reclined relatives, contemplative and nostalgic.

The world wounds. It opens into great crevasses seemingly everywhere people need to step. And what with gravity, it's too easy to trip and fall in. But right then, they were there; between them, four generations, so it was all right. Even with the wounds, all right.

He had just asked, was granted permission, and sat down.

For a while they just looked into their coffees, stirred in their sugar, and smiled sheepishly at the circumstance. So young, their experiences in courtship were malformed, infantile, filled with hope and missteps. He'd walked into the diner only moments before, ordered a coffee at the bar, and turned to see her, sitting alone, a book spread in front of her on the table, a cup of coffee steaming beside it. It was as if he couldn't help himself; that face radiated such a light, the skin seeming to ask for his fingertips. He had never been very cavalier, but it was one of those moments, one of those times in life when a person truly realizes that they stand upon a crossroads, an intersection where the next second determines the rest of their lives. He knew it. It was now or never, this moment or no moment, everything or nothing; so he took up his coffee, went over, asked to join her, was granted permission, and sat.

Before them was only a few feet of white table, but what was really before them was the Universe, everything, an endless pearled string of moments that, despite there being only so many, could go on and on in the perfection that rewarded his courage to walk up. Just walk up and say hello. Can I sit? And in such a simple act, such an everyday thing, something forged that no foundry could emulate. And it was this: two people sat across from one another and breathed a common air that they would always know, and always love. They looked up from their coffees at one another.

On a jukebox in the corner, a quiet song came on:

But the cat came back
The very next day.
The cat came back,
I thought he was a goner
But the cat came back,
He just wouldn't stay away.

"I'm Harold," he said.
"Madeline."

Seeing Bones

When I saw Edward again, the first time in ten years, the bartender at the open bar filled his wine glass halfway with Johnny Walker Black, and he said to me, "Ever since rehab, I know my limits." He held the stem of the glass and pivoted it with the perfectness of physics to allow the contents into his mouth. The wedding was in that purgatorial-time, stuck vortex-like between the big cathedral ceremony and the introduction of the parties at the country club reception, which meant a lot of expensively priced but undercooked hors d'oeuvres and a lot of awkward conversation with estranged extended family. And an open bar.

My wife, Elaine, and I were the kind of people who'd left where they were from: went to college and found the nearest big city to forget heart-palpitating words like "rural" or the "suburbs." One predictable result was that we'd lost contact with a lot of the people we grew up with, like siblings. Like my second cousin, Edward. And so on the occasions when marital ceremonies or deaths brought the black sheep back from their urban hideouts to reconnect with their more prosaic pasts, there was a lot of confrontational pretending. There was the strange, human happening of seeing the image you had of a younger friend changed irrevocably by the foolish mandatory nature of seeing them again in all of their adult shortcomings.

Edward was seated at our table, the emptiness of his plus-one more profound by the clothed and bow-ornamented chair to his right, on which no one sat. We waited for the bouncing bridal parties to bound in, awkwardly in the dresses and tuxedos they weren't used to wearing, and sipped our drinks in what seemed more like gulps: the neverendingness of open bars opening throats. Elaine, meeting Edward for the first time, asked the perfunctory questions of new acquaintances that were family but that did not have the blood of family—sisters and brothers and cousins all in the black ink of legalese.

"So, Edward, what do you do?"

"I'm in nuclear medicine."

My eyes dropped to the table.

"Which means, I work in imaging," he continued. "So basically, I do the X-Rays."

"That's very interesting," she said, the ability of hers to make every dis-ingenuousness sound true.

"Yeah. You know. It's money."

Propelled by my own generously-filled glass, I thought, only, of bad puns: *Edward, a ward of his own Education.*

Cousin, a sinful coup.

Liquor, but what if she licks you first?

My family frowned upon our living in a big city—a big plane ride away—and were simultaneously in awe that we were a part of what Edward would later call, "A rat king where the most interesting humans wove their tails." (I was taken by his crass poetry).

"So, where are your little ones?" Edward asked. The middle-aged DJ searched his laptop playlist for his presumptions of what club music was then the most popular. If he succeeded, I didn't know, lost as I was, too, at understanding what pleased the youngest in the room. All I heard under Edward's question was thumping and what sounded like someone strangling electricity.

"Home," Elaine said. "We have a friend watching them."

"All weekend?"

"Well, for the couple days we're here. It's okay. They know our friends and our friends know them."

"That's cool," Edward said, his feelings of the preposterousness of city life gleaned only from the tail end of his words' resonance.

"The thing is," I said, "You can't bring them. As in, you can't take them. Anywhere. I mean," and here's where the loose tongue wriggles itself right out of the mouth; here's where Elaine's glare hid, only kind of, the fear she had that I hated our children, "Once you have them, it's like they have you. Always. That whole being an independent, self-serving, icon of freedom goes kaput." Kaput. I never said words like *kaput*. Edward's face had the look of those who were nostalgic about children because they didn't have them and wondered if they were too old to have them. It was also the same look that betrayed, in the non-parent, that they had no solitary clue what it meant to raise a child.

I caught Elaine's glare, knowing it was there all along, then sputtered, "But it's also, like, the greatest thing in the entire world, Edward. Truly." Paternal credentials met.

We hadn't invited Edward to our wedding. Most of our extended family, burrowed as they were in domestically-converted farmhouses with too many rooms for too few or in endlessly replicated vinyl-sided cul-de-sac monstrosities just outside real metropolitan areas, were—likewise—not invited. We were not rude people. Our goal wasn't to ostracize our family. Rather, our mistake was insisting that our wedding—that our lives—were our own things; that we wanted to do things our way. That, in a world where being selfish was such a pejorative, at least our wedding would be our own. We were younger then, not yet parents, and so did not realize our lives were very far from "our own things." The subsequent decade, the real indicator of a marriage's longevity ("the hardest years," my aunt had said, at her 30th anniversary), we had to deal with our guilt and our families' chagrin at not being at our very special, very unique, own, day. That I didn't, at the very least, reserve a dance for my mother.

Edward had yet to meet our children. They were as elusive to him as characters in a story he didn't have the patience to read, but he still had the thoughtfulness to ask after them. Our estrangement—Edward's and mine—began just before Elaine and I were married, at a Christmas party I'd come home to attend where I saw him do a line of cocaine (for the first time) from the porcelain of his parents' washroom's toilet tank and I drove drunk (for the only time) back to the hotel to get away from it. As urban as I'd become, I was still rather urbane in the whitewashed suburban conformity of my rearing. Turns out, his snorting was to become more than recreational.

"That's good," Edward said, in reaction to my histrionic parenting, then took a drink that made his throat bob the way a jaw pulses at its hinge when clenched. "I look forward to having some, someday. Kids."

And then, they came. The bridesmaids, the groomsmen.

The uniformity of the peach-beige dresses; the exactitude of the black-tux redundancy. The bride and groom, man and wife, the I-Doers, in all the majesty of over-indulgence, highlighting and underscoring in vicious detail how much Elaine and I had shortchanged our families from the bad dancing and roaring drunkenness that was their right for sharing our blood. The DJ passed a hand through his thinning, dyed hair in a way he'd certainly learned from studying the day's heartthrobs, and mispronounced the difficult Italian names of the groomsmen. No matter, they strutted in, patriarchal elbows crooked for the ladies' taking, and gesticulated curiously for the benefit of the rented cameraman. And at that moment, thinking all of these things, I realized a certain level of my own jadedness. My judgmental instinct emphasized by the genuineness of Edward's smile, as he watched the procession glide, happily, by.

I first realized I was not the father I intended to be on the day I took my son to the Museum of Art to see my favorite painting by James Jacques Tissot and he didn't care about it. He was six, and so probably didn't rightfully need to grasp what joy the inane portrait brought to his charlatan father. But I was teaching him the badly-enunciated first-year French I knew, the Grimm's, addition, the proper techniques for bouldering on our furniture—in short, I was doing all I could to raise the genius he'd need to be to both take and challenge the conventions of our ever-frustrating world. I was antagonistic to the redundant maxim that non-parents had (that perhaps I had before becoming a parent): *I wouldn't want to bring a child into this world*. It was too reductive and non-pragmatic; I didn't want the species to end. I only thought it best to raise a child with enough cerebral ingenuity to justify my own curiosity (see: ineptitude) at making a substantive change to our collective human lot.

Was it a lot to ask that we bypass the dinosaurs at the Academy of Natural Sciences for just one day in order to see French portraiture?

"You see the detail, Elliot?"

"Yeah."

"It's amazing, isn't it?"

"Yeah, Daddy."

Elliot was a precocious but respectful kid; he benefited from his parents' insisting that formal education was an anemic supplement to what we would teach him at home. He also benefited from the wild diversity of the city. Our picnicking in public parks, museum membershipping, and worldly food trying (et al) was buttressed by the endless redacting we had to do in explaining to him and his sister why the strange people of the city did their strange things. High high art.

Though he responded with the appropriate pseudo-gusto, I could see he was not nearly as interested in the painting as I was. His little eyes flitted to the other walls with childlike ennui. And this painting, this portrait of whoever by a painter whose other work I hadn't ever seen, stalled me, years ago, the first time I'd gone there, and had done so every time since. If only there to see a traveling exhibit, I'd make sure to stop by to—I don't know—say hi. To visit. Alone on the wall for what seemed forever, I felt it was the least I could do to stop by. Pay my respects. Sign the guest registry.

He needed to understand.

"But, Elliot. Look at how real these things look even though they're not."

"But they were real, Dad. He painted them."

"But. Oh. But he could have painted them from his imagination."

"Did he, Dad?"

I didn't know. In all the years, I didn't do the research; stuck as I was in the nostalgic emotionalism of "visiting" my painting, I didn't want scholarly research to besmirch my experience. What would I do if I found out the portrait was of a slumlord public menace or that Tissot was a pedophile? "No. Probably not, Elliot. He probably painted it from real life. But still, that's not easy. What I mean is, can you see how amazing it is that Tissot was able to capture this scene in this way?"

"Yeah, I can see it."

"But not just see it, Elliot. Feel it. When you stand there, right at this spot, can you feel the painting?"

"I'm not standing, though, Dad."

It was true; I had lifted him to see the painting up close. Slumping at the shoulders, I lowered Elliot to the ground and said "Nevermind" in the way that was supposed to elicit pity, but word tonality was something I forgot to teach him in our home.

When he ambled over to the bronze in the middle of the room and I followed, I turned to look back at the Tissot, knowing I would never again see it in the same light. From then on, when I went there, the memory of Elliot's not feeling what I felt would cover the spot like a veil. Like the painting itself was drapery-covered in some old French attic, forgotten like the bogus melodramatic emotion it elicited in me.

Oh, how I wished I could change my son.

Weddings: the elaborate beginnings we think them to be, but also so close to webbings, where you're stuck for a bit before being eaten. My bad puns as endless as the bar.

Someone had a checklist (the Maid of Honor? The DJ?) listing all the itemized, perfunctory elements of the festivities. The cake sliced, the slices face-smashed. The dancing, melodramatic up to and including hysterical tears. The *Electric Slide*, slid. The stuttered speeches of the inebriate head table. The chicken *and* the fish. We were halfway through the ghastly tradition of some stranger sliding a garter up the trembling, goose-pimpled, naked leg of the most athletic of the single girls when Elaine tugged a little at the sleeve by my triceps and asked, "Where's Edward?" I looked around and, in not finding the object of the query, shrugged. I turned back to watch the blush of the girl's face as the garter-pusher's upper arms disappeared under her skirt and his sinister smile widened, but was now distracted. I, too, wanted to know where Edward had gone. There's something fascinating about reconnection, even under the temporary and prescribed circumstances of a wedding; in all of the expectations of the past, there seemed only scant traces that resembled a person you knew, like fingerprints beginning to lose their rings. I didn't know Edward any longer; he didn't know me. But we shared a history, which meant we owed something. Whether we liked it or not, the compunction that drove us to understand one another was buried permanent where our roots crossed.

"Dance with me," Elaine said, smiling. "It's not like we get out that often. Remember when we used to dance?" The question fumed of old-speech, like something you were supposed to say to a spouse of many decades, near the end of your mutual existences. It wasn't all that long ago that we danced.

She nodded over to the parquet dance floor, where the prototypical commonplaceness of the festivities had ceded to a swarm of people swaying like heat distortions over pavement: the once-in-a-while where people who never danced (who had no business dancing), danced.

"You want to dance to club music?"

"Could be fun."

"Let's wait for a slow song, Elaine."

"They only play like two slow songs at weddings anymore." She said this to me but it was as if she'd said it to no one.

"Next slow one, I promise."

"What are you worried about?"

"In dancing to this?"

"Yeah."

"I don't know. That. Looking like that." I nodded toward the horde.

"No one cares."

The thumping thumped on, and we sat there alone at the table. Elaine must have been thinking about our children and I was certainly thinking about our children, but together, we were only thinking of the children in relation to ourselves—what they meant, even in being their own people, to *our* lives. It was as if being a parent made you simultaneously the most selfless and selfish thing. We wanted them to have everything, but we carefully defined that everything within the parameters of our own paradigms.

"Let me see if I can find Edward," I said to Elaine, rising with my glass; thinking better of it, putting the glass down.

I saw him from the balcony of the clubhouse. He was walking across the ninth green of the golf course. I wasn't sure if it was the ninth but I liked to think of it as such: halfway through. I hurried.

He had stopped just beyond the cup and sat down. I found out his relationship to the cup because, as I approached, the ball of my foot plummeted in the nothingness of it and I sprained my ankle, sprawling to the ground behind him and eliminating any hope of stealth.

"Aren't there supposed to be damned yellow flags?" I moaned, rolling in perhaps too childish a fashion for my innocuous injury.

"Are you okay?" Edward asked, rising to come to my aid.

"Yes. I suppose," I responded, through with the spectacle. "Let me just sit with you." He sat back down and I crawled over to join him. "What are you doing out here?"

"Nothing. Just catching my breath."

"You feeling okay?"

"I am. You?"

"All but the ankle."

"Bartender's generous."

"People tip big at weddings. It's all the euphoria and nostalgia," I said.

"Yeah."

The course was illuminated with the orange sodium vapor of the lamps. A sand trap, a ways away, cut like a pock mark into an otherwise perfectly spherical green mound of the adjacent hole. Caught in this way, the scene before us, stretching in undulations of land so manicured it couldn't be true, our environment was quietly part of us. When we breathed, it went into our blood, that shared blood of vague familiarity. Somehow, in ways neither of us understood, there were elements of his blood that were the same in my blood, and that basic fact was important. We made it important: blood's viscosity trumping water somehow central to our human condition. Somehow. I never used words like *somehow*. They reminded me of how little I understood anything.

"You still like living in the city?" Edward asked. Then he said that thing about the rat king.

"I do. It's hectic. It's loud. But it has a lot of advantages."

"Elliot and…and…"

"Suzanne."

"Elliot and Suzanne don't mind not having a yard or anything?"

"The neighborhood has parks, Edward. They're better than a yard," I said, mistaking his basic questioning for accusation. "And anyway, I don't have to mow them," I said, recovering.

He laughed. "So, what's it like? Living in a big city and coming back here to this?"

I hadn't realized it until he asked, but the phenomenon he spoke of happened to have been a major focus of my unconscious thought until it surfaced with his question. I suppose I had been musing about my return here all day, "It feels like I've found El Dorado. Or Atlantis. You know? I feel like I went out and I found Atlantis. And the other people in the city, they don't even know they can breathe under water. That they *are* breathing under water. And I come here and it's like everyone is afraid of drowning. That's what it was like when I moved to the city from the suburbs, that I realized how to breathe under water. Is that too complex a metaphor?"

"No. I may stand around radiation all day, but I'm not an idiot."

"Sorry. I'm drunk."

"Don't apologize. *I'm* drunk."

We both laughed out at the golf course.

"I was just remembering when we were kids," Edward said. "You remember sleepovers? We'd stay up all night watching Godzilla trying not to get caught."

"I think it was like one in the morning."

"What was?"

"How late we actually stayed up."

"Felt like all night," he said.

"Yeah."

I hadn't noticed it at first, but the sounds from the clubhouse behind us seemed to amplify; there was either a wedding reception or a prison break in congress. Edward's gaze out upon the course reminded me of Elliot's when he was caught with thinking; perhaps there was something to family. Maybe there *was* eternity in progeny.

"Godzilla," he said again, reflectively.

"Yeah."

There's a sweet injustice to what was.

How quickly a year goes.

How quickly all the years go.

"You know, it's been fifteen years now that I've been taking X-Rays."

"Wow, Edward. That's great. That's a hell of a long time. That's really something. That's…" It's frustrating, sometimes, to talk.

"No. I mean, what I'm saying is…I'm just not there anymore. I don't really want to be there. What I mean is…when I think of the city, where people are, where people are doing things…and I'm in that hospital, the same room, every day. Pushing the same button. Asking people the same questions. Seeing their bones."

"But you're making good money, right?"

"That's the thing, isn't it? The presumed safety of easy decisions."

Behind: the revel, rabbling, rabid.

"I went to college," he continued, "because you were supposed to go to college. The lore was, if you don't go to college, you're going to end up at McDonald's. That's what we thought, back then. Hell, it's probably what they still think today. You either go to college and get a degree and make money or you end up in some terrible situation. Vague, but terrible."

"That's what my parents told me," I offered.

"Me too. My dad had this fear in his eyes when he talked to me. He was very stern when we talked about college, about what I wanted to *do* with my life, like my life was a thing I would act on and not just something I had. Like everyone, I had no idea what I was supposed to *do*, but that look in his eye scared me. I thought I might be some Bohemian writer. He told me I had to go to college and choose a major that would make me money. He asked what in the Hell I could do studying literature. So it made sense back then: two-year degree, instant job making pretty decent money. Thing is, no one ever tells you there's a lot of life to live while making money. No one ever says there might be other things to think about. So I work the same shift on the same days, making all of that money, surviving, and all the time, the fear in my dad's eyes looks at me the way he did. And the thing is, I see that fear when I look at my own, now, in a reflection. There they are, my dad's eyes, afraid and looking at me, but scared of the wrong thing. All along, scared of the wrong thing. I know there's more than the bones that I see, but they're all I see, anymore."

"But, you know, Edward. That's his job, as a father, you know. To make sure you survive. And look at you. You're alive."

"So that's being a father," Edward said, more to himself than to the ether, or me. I didn't know what kind of convincing I was trying to do. Edward's life, mired to suburbanism, handcuffed to drone capital, made me think of empty but beautiful things: canyons, pupils. But I wanted to make him feel better. I wanted him to think he could go back to school, major in English, move to the city. Grow a beard. But here was the reality: we were two old cousins sitting on a golf course, my children far away in a big city, and his father sitting somewhere with fear in his eyes. Tomorrow would be the first day in the years that would separate us again before the next wedding or funeral. I'd fly home. He'd drive to work and look into the insides of people. Edward didn't do anything wrong, and yet how else could it feel?

I wondered, sitting there, what sort of emotion my eyes betrayed to my children; what Elliot saw when the emptiness of my pupils filled with himself. We have no idea what the vibrations of a chord we strike might mean to those outside our instrument.

When I returned to the reception hall, I saw the bride and groom thanking Elaine for coming while looking over to the next guest to thank. I wondered if they asked where I was. I wondered if they knew who she was.

The wedding was winding down and I was reminded of the gentle dusks of the city when things were almost quiet. As in, the only sounds were the planes overhead and the sirens that didn't even cause us alarm anymore, as much wolf as they cried. On evenings like that I could watch the clouds on my back patio, bounce Elliot and Suzanne on my knees in the most stereotypical fashion that still felt perfect, smell the dog piss from the neighbor's adjacent, attached patio, and feel for a second just right—before the sun set and it was dark and the peculiar night sounds of the city set in.

The bride and groom moved on to someone else they didn't recognize and Elaine turned to see me. I limped back to her, my ankle swelling under its strain.

"What did you do?" she asked.

"Went golfing."

She cocked her head puppy-like and I held out my hand.

"You're going to dance to club music hobbled like that?"

"I won't look any sillier than anyone else," I responded.

We went to the dance floor and became heat distortions amidst the strangled electricity.

It occurred to me briefly that Edward could look deep into my ankle, see me inside. Maybe he couldn't diagnose the grade of the sprain, but he could see my bones, naked as they appear only to those closest to us, regardless of any distance.

Grey Island (IX-XI)

BOOM!
Crackle.
Steel screech. Bend. Buckle. Hold. Warm.
Twinkle tinkles. Shard shower.
Rustle. Hurried clutter.
This way that way.
Looming unillimunated EXIT stairwell sign.
Brrrrrrrrrr bend.
Silence.
Shout.
"What?!"
"!!"
Bump, tumble, knee red scrape.
Rise.
Cry.
Banshee wail against the fire whoosh.
"Little girl, where are your parents?"
Wail.

Blue balloon, rising. Away with gravity.
Up up up.
Out the open window.
I watch.
Blue balloon. Up.
Knee scrape.
Ouch. Wail.
Balloon. Small. Blue jay.
Gone.

My dress, red at the knee.
"Your parents?"
Wail.
I stand.
Rushing. Everything. Fast. Quick moves, startle.
Quick breaths, black smoke.
Cough.

Hot. Heating.

Up.

Tall birds, ties and shirt tails, flying from the windows.

Noise.

"It's too loud. It's too loud!"

"Come this way. Come with me, sweetheart."

"It's too loud! It's too loud!"

Run.

Run back.

Run forth.

Stop.

Ledge. Edge. Down. Snowing.

It's snowing.

Smile. Christmas.

Not cold.

Lifted from behind.

Another shout. "Come on!"

"Christmas!"

"What?"

"Christmas!"

"No."

Squirm. Put down. Voice gone.

Growl. Stone rumble.

Fire below.

Ouch knee. Touch red running. Ouch!

Wail.

Stop. Breathe. Smoke. Cough.

Turn. Turn again. Turn.

Flashes of color. Stung eyes.

Close. Burn.

Water.

"Don't leave me. Wait for me. Wait."

Quiet voice. Soundless. Scream. Nothing.

Falling.

Rising.

More BOOM.

More.

Grind squeal bend. Snap. Hot.

Roar. Animals.

Roaring.
Trip. Hands palms glass. Ouch.

Exit door return.
"Trapped!"
"What?"
"Trapped!"
"No."
"Yes. Below. Fire"
"Blocked?"
"Yes."
"Up?"
"Maybe."
I am quiet. Mommy says to be quiet.
Mommy.
Where?
I look. No.
Corner. I sit.
Quiet.
Man comes.
Sits.
"Hello."
I look.
"Are you okay?"
I look.
"Let me see."
Knee. Ouch.
"Ooo. It's okay. No big deal."
Smiles. I look.
Mommy?
"Mommy?"
"Mommy? Do you know where your mommy is?"
"Mommy?"
Looks around.
"Okay."

Cannot see.
Man puts something over my face.
I move.
He holds. I move.

"It's okay. Relax."
Noise noise noise.
Ouch.
Shaking the world. Moving. Back and forth.
Earthquake.
The ground. Grumbling. Hungry stomach.
The building is hungry.
Let's feed it.
Stop the rumbling.
Okay?
I am not scared.
Thump thump thump. Crack.
Now orange.
Orange bright. I remember camping.
Marshmallows and sticks.
And hot. So hot.
Summer snow.
Orange everywhere. Shout. Ouch. Scream.
I don't.
I'm up. Man's arms.
Running.
Orange everywhere. Grumbling stomach still.
Licking orange up.
Growing from grumbling ground.
Hot flowers blooming.
I reach to touch.
"No. No. Sweetheart."
Knee against his side. Ouch.
Orange glow, smoke darkened. Short breath.
"It's okay. It's okay. It's okay."
Quick breaths, I feel the heart.
The heart and voice, "It's okay. It's okay. God."
God.
He smiles.

Stairs bumping. Up.
I hold hard. His hair.
Shoulders.

Bounce like Daddy.
A daddy.
Where?
Open bright, rush.
Brisk cold bright open light wide out.
Out. Outside.
Tall birds, arms waving.
Waving down. And up.
Waving wild, side to side.
Dive.
I wave too.
My arms, flapping. Taking off.
Man stops. Down sitting roof.
I flap to fly.
He smiles.
"Bird?"
"Bird."
"Can you fly?"
I nod.

Shaking. Vibrations. Orange rumble.
"What are they doing?"
"No!"
Bird tumble.
"No!"
My knee doesn't hurt.
My hands black. I rub them together.
The black comes off. Is there again.
"It'll be over soon."
Man smiling. Sitting. Looking.
I look at him.
My black hands.
I rub one against his cheek. Black streak.
"They'll probably send a helicopter to get us."
Loud bending.
Steal twist squeal sequel.
Dip tip.
All standing fall.

"What?"
"The whole thing! Down!"
"No! It can't."
"It can."

People on knees.
Lips moving.
Silent.
Hands together. Now I lay me down to sleep.
I say.
Clasped hands again too.
Man does too.
I pray the Lord my soul to keep.
He says too.
Fun.
Same time.
If I die before I wake.
Cough.
I pray the Lord my soul to take.
"Good."

Cough cough cough.
Hair pushed back. Stays stuck.
Adults crying.
Sad.
Poor poor poor them.
"Where?"
"The second."
"Another?"
"Yes. Oh!!"
"!!"
"Oh my God!"
"Falling?"
"Yes."
"No!"
People run.
People stand still.
Hugging. Crying.
Crackle. Bend. Groan.
Tired angry. Groan.

Black smoke balloons with strings.
Playing with the sky.
So many.
Cough.

Loud sound.
"What's your name?"
Look. Quiet.
"It's okay. What's your name?"
Smile. Sitting.
There. Roof. Squeal.
Banshee wail.
Nothing.
Crack. Snap. BOOM!
We shake.
Rumble. I hum.
Hmmmmm mm m mmm mmmm mmmm m.
Haha.
Haha.
"What's your name?"
"I'm not supposed to talk to strangers."
Haha.
Haha.
We know.
Haha.

Bend.
Melt.
Orange and black up and up.
Grey snow shards down to the grey island.
Grey stone brick glass.
Grey rivers.
Grey black and grey white.
Alone island.
Grey smoking black balloons.
Snow and big birds falling.
It's okay.
It's grey.
Faces.
Afraid. I'm not.

I say, "I'm not."
"Not what?"
We shout.
"Afraid."
Man looks. Coughs.
So curious.
Cries. A little. Quiet cry only.
His face, grey.

Daytime dark.
Street people below.
I wave.
No.
Two rivers.
Bridges all across.
It stopped moving.
All of it.
Groan.
Yellow cabs parked.
Frozen island. Shhhh.
It's almost time for bed.
Morning but bedtime.
Nap.
Goodnight grey island.
Shhhh.
So still. Tired. Sleep.
Yawn.
Stretch.
Noon nap.
Bedtime story.
Wake in my own bed. My sheets.
My friends.
Dreams. Pretty and scary.
Tonight.

All around. Movement.
Hustle. Rustle. Sweep and change.
The man scoots closer.
"Hold my hand. It's okay."
"What?"

"What's okay?"
I nod.
"I don't know. Everything, I suppose."
Everything's okay.
Okay.
I believe him.
I reach out my hand.
So many birds and balloons.

Brrrrrrr buckle.
Jolt. Stutter.
Tip. Tree in wind.
Hurricane.
Breathe cough.
Man holds my shoulders.
Looks at my eyes.
I look at his.
Stares.
Seconds minutes.
Smile.
Smile.
"Well."
Sitting us. I'm not scared.
"Are you scared?"
I shake.
My head.
"Good."
He points. Up.
"Look."
Through the black. The smoke.
A hole. Clouds.
White. Big. Beautiful.
Sky. Blue.
Day. Today.
Crumble. Shaking.
Gravity.
Down down down.
Man grabs.
"Look."
Points up.

Sky. Cloud. Further.
"Just watch that."
Smoke covers again.
Grey island.
Goodnight.
!!
ii

Grab

On a small side-street in a small side-city, Patrick "Hawk" Awkly was about fifty feet behind the woman and not paying much attention when she fell forward and hard against the sidewalk. By the time he was able to reach her, the blood from her head wound had slithered into a petite, somehow perfectly round puddle; the flow had stopped but it was enough to startle him as he knelt beside her, looking at her aslant in the chaos that thrusts one so far from normalcy that the most obvious and appropriate reaction escapes the victim.

He had received the "Hawk" moniker in high school, though there was nothing truly hawk-like about him. He had, in fact, poor eyesight, which resulted in his having to wear thick-cut lenses in the framed glasses affixed too-tightly to his temples (there were pressure marks). He wasn't aggressive nor majestic nor sky-tested nor wild; Patrick was one of those unremarkable people that made up the very vast majority of all people, who, eventually, grew out of the juvenile pursuit of celebrity in favor of a more grounded banality. There was a profound tranquility in being unknown and basic that the aging feared but accepted placidly. It was only his last name that provoked his classmates into the obligatory malapropism.

He immediately noticed that the woman was both young and very pretty. In her late twenties, Patrick was likely a decade her senior, and the thought of it intimidated him (despite her being unconscious). It was not often that he interacted with such women and it felt to him almost a trespass, even though he was doing little more than kneeling beside her and calling an ambulance from his phone. He felt of himself not particularly unattractive, but more so in-between the polarities of attraction—he was beyond the arrogant confidence of youth and before the maturity of wizened years, where the body and all its bones settle like the sturdy foundations of an august house. He was, then, stuck in the chasm of awkwardness in trying to maintain what was no longer there while wrestling with the acknowledgment that his before-had charms worked no more wonders on the opposite sex. He was widening and seemingly shrinking—a terrible combined prospect— and there was less hair and more face lines; in short, playing the accidental hero for the young woman was a unwarranted boost to his fragile ego, warped as it was by the reality of a timeline that ran only one way. The side-street was devoid of anyone else and Patrick wished for her to awaken, to fixate through the concussed fog upon him for a second, if only to identify the one stranger that was there for her.

It felt like he couldn't help it. He noticed what she was wearing: a white, button-up blouse that form-fitted her athletically thin torso; a grey, frieze skirt too-warm for the season but, again, fitted well; black stockings; and black heels. A handbag splayed its insides a few sidewalk slabs away, flung in the plummet. Patrick felt ashamed; that poor young woman, hurt who knew how bad, her blood the sort of thick no one ever expects it to be, darkening the place it had congregated outside of her body (he made careful not to disturb it; would it help the paramedics diagnose her trauma?), and there he was, looking at the flattering way her clothes fit her body. What drew him to think the thought? To look? To, he would never say it aloud, imagine?

Emergency call made, Patrick waited for the ambulance to arrive. No other pedestrian appeared—it was, he remembered, early morning, that strange city time when a busy place is still before the rush of people—and he felt compelled to soothe her somehow. He took her right hand in his and placed his left on her shoulder. It was benign, an inert gesture that served to comfort him more than her, but it felt right to do so. There, suffering, was another human being in need of compassion, and it seemed to him the responsibility of each to provide for any other in such a circumstance. Patrick wore the badge of himself.

With his respective hands engaged at her hand and shoulder, his sight was drawn to the inconspicuous rise of her right breast, which undulated slowly with her restful breath in the firm cup of a bra. He scrunched his nose at himself, furrowed his brow at the horror, but looked nevertheless. There was no one present. She was unaware of anything. It hurt, he reasoned, no one, for him to look. He shook his head at himself—the poor girl—and looked closely. How long until the paramedics arrived?

Patrick loved his wife but always wondered if he could have done better. She was pretty but not beautiful. Thin but not skinny. Smart but not deep. A wonderful partner but could there have been better? And her breasts, once her great attraction for him, had become what breasts become. He knew, truly, that he would never leave her (maybe because she would never leave him) and so in that certainty he felt a sense of freedom in imagining his life with another. He concocted elaborate fantasies of his wife dying young, premature, of some vague illness—cancer seemed ready—so that he, the mourning widower not yet too old, could find his head in the lap of some younger, prettier, skinnier, smarter, more wonderful girl. The thoughts always disturbed him and ended abruptly with a cleansing return to reality, but they returned as readily as the following day and he was there to meet them—another girl in passing, the quintessential potential. Patrick was realistic with himself (not even waitresses flirted with him anymore) but the idea stuck: the if of it all.

Patrick removed his right hand from the fallen girl's and placed it on her breast.

It happened so quickly that he scarcely even recognized he'd done it. His hand was there, rising upon the breast with each of her inhalations. He knew it was wrong yet did not remove it. In that early morning, the side-street still abandoned, no ambulance siren in earshot, Patrick left his hand inert there. She would never know, he knew, and no one looked. It was a thing that wasn't done but he was doing it and beyond its wrongness it felt like what Patrick believed he deserved. Somewhere in the world of his current self, he believed there was a buried him to which he owed the small open pleasure with no recourse. There, there was no law, no ethics or propriety, no one was hurt. It was an inanimate object that he took for his in his hand because he had a right to seize to himself the things he could command with the boldness of his will. Men like him, he thought clandestinely, perhaps all men, were taught to grab at their target, to pull toward themselves whatever they wanted, because the world was invented for their taking, and Patrick was tired of not meeting his own expectations.

He heard the siren that seemed simultaneously far off and around the corner, as screams do.

And Awkly released his talons.

It was gone. She was gone. No name. The ambulance had rounded a corner in route to the nearest hospital and in the intervening space between the uncanny and the rote, Patrick stood rigidly next to the drying pool of blood. The day had awakened and pedestrians began passing him in the histrionic voracity of people late for work, rushing into buildings to sit. None of them knew what had just occurred: the fall nor the trespass. It concerned Patrick how ignorant the people were to what had happened in that very space only minutes ago; a fellow person had fallen and injured herself and only because they were slower or because their workday started later, they would never know it had happened. To them, on their commute, the world was as it always was. But to Patrick, it had encountered a friction that prevented him from joining the hoard in their advancement toward the typical.

He'd *had* to do it. That was the thing, he thought, he did not have a choice. Something primitive, primal. It was animalistic and biological. Who was he to challenge blood and evolution and the deeply sewn, maybe God-inflicted need to reproduce? He was Patrick Awkly, not strong enough to deny society nor culture in how they'd conspired to construct him.

Patrick began walking; it was amazing how quickly the current of the crowd accepted him. In the vast anonymity of that community, no one could see the stain on his hand. His face bore the same struggling workday scowl of everyone in the country that morning, so in the oscillation of his justification and his shame, he was safe from the scrutiny of the others.

He got to his building and entered at its entrance and rode its elevator and opened the glass doors of his office and negotiated the hallways of his company and found his cubical and sat in his chair at his desk with his computer and pens and telephone and no window and the cushy pad for under his feet. He exhaled a breath into the place that collected such exhales for days and years.

What else could he do? He worked. His job was the sort of unremarkable that it served him no real purpose to even care to describe it. When, in meeting someone, he was asked the obligatory *what do you do?* in the American way that sounded like *how do you spend your human life?* but actually meant *how do you make money to legitimize your existence?*, he didn't know how to respond. He knew the details of his job but didn't know how to explain them to a new acquaintance without it sounding like an automatic bore, a purposeless task that screamed at the other person: I've sacrificed all raw passion for a life on cruise control.

He couldn't help thinking that his coworkers knew. With every glance or side-comment, Patrick swore they'd somehow seen, knew him for what he really was. The dentist can tell if you don't floss, even if you've flossed that day.

Their discourse was always focused on the mundanities of their work world together, but that day felt different; Patrick knew that there were parts of himself that had just revealed themselves for the first time. It frightened him to know there were likely parts still yet to be discovered. As he went through the items of his work, he thought of the sexual harassment training in which his company forced him to participate every couple of years. There was a computer program wherein the employee would read a series of obvious, over-the-top slides then take a short exam proving that they'd understood right from wrong. (Example: Eric tells Vanessa he can get her a promotion if she agrees to perform fellatio on him in a supply closet. Is *this* an example of an inappropriate work scenario?). The rub of the exam was, no matter how many questions you got wrong, you could simply read an auxiliary explanation for your wrong choice and pass the test. (Example: You chose *no*, Eric was not wrong in proposing oral sex to Vanessa. The correct answer was *yes*. Vanessa may feel uncomfortable knowing her success is linked to performing sex acts on male coworkers). Every couple of years, Patrick could hit the *next* arrow at the bottom of each slide in rapid succession, take the exam by answering correctly all of the obvious questions and selecting *next* after the auxiliary incorrect answers, and print out his certificate of completion for the mandatory sexual harassment training at work and be off the hook for a few more years. And his company couldn't be sued.

Just after lunch, a coworker approached Patrick at his cubical and told him he had a visitor. He had given one of the paramedics his information but had forgotten immediately that he'd done so. The prospect before him seemed a universal reckoning, the Big Bang laughing at his spec of littleness as it lashed its fate at him with a bullwhip. Unconscious, yes, but clearly the young woman was aware enough to know what he'd done; the police were now here to confront him about his offense and to arrest him on charges of sexual assault. The survivalist in his soul flooded him with adrenaline and his lunch dropped, but somewhere else—in that vague locale of conscience—he felt the scales of justice regain their equilibrium. In the way the guilty feel half-good when near-caught, he'd run from the trap but kept a toe behind by giving the paramedics his name, the name of his company, by pointing ambiguously in the direction of his building. Patrick tried to put on a brave face and readied his wrists for cuffs.

When she hugged him he didn't dare breathe.

"It's just..." she said. "I'm so..." She hugged him again.

Patrick patted her back just between the shoulder blades in the most platonic way possible; his coworkers were all looking, smiling the grins of colleagues who'd never thought to know him outside of work but were proud to know they shared an office with such a caliber of person. She withdrew and he noticed that she was wearing the same outfit. The blouse—he refused to look at it. He could barely look to her eyes—all of that gunpowder in the bullets of beautiful women. On her head was a bandage already bled-through.

"It was a concussion," she said. "God damn heels." Jesus, he thought, did it have to be a stereotype? What was her name? He couldn't ask; it seemed sinister to know it. "Listen, I'm really grateful that you stayed and helped me. It's hard not to be cynical in the city, everyone walking by people without caring about them." Tears, actual tears, threatened to breech and Patrick wondered if she'd close in to embrace him again. "They didn't want to but I made them tell me who'd helped me after I woke up."

"Patrick," he said, extending his hand in awkward non-sequitur, introducing himself. She looked confused for a moment, then took it. Perhaps that *was* the charming thing to do: disarm her vulnerability and make like they'd just met. He thought about asking what she *did*. Her hand met his hand. He withdrew it maybe too quickly.

"Hi, Patrick," she said, then gave her own name. He forgot it instantly.

The rest of the interchange was curt, a little bizarre, but full of what anyone would expect to hear between someone who'd been done an altruistic service and the scoundrel who'd done it. Perhaps she was still loopy in the concussion haze, Patrick thought. All the better. Maybe I can get her number, ask her for coffee. My wife could get cancer. No.

When she left and his coworkers scattered, Patrick went back to his desk and sat down. The things around him were his things, his unremarkable things, but they carried a new charge of weakness. The stapler wasn't strong enough to compress its discarded metal tines. He had reveled in the celebration of his lie and Patrick sunk into the emptiness of that celebrity; he knew the vacancy of getting what you didn't deserve when you took what was never yours to begin with.

She'd had a name, at least, he thought.

Despite the fact that Patrick could never concisely explain what he did at work—something to do with reports of call logs to providers of consultants—he returned home each evening shouldering the weight of exhaustion. It was as if the inertness of office life was more taxing on the body than strenuous exercise. Oh, those professional athletes, Patrick thought, who must rest so easily in the over-exertion of their belabored bodies. No one truly knew the fatigue associated with monotonous micro-movements (fingers tapping, eyes blinking); except of course, for those occupying similar shapes in similar spaces in the adjacent buildings—stone and glass walls notwithstanding, Patrick knew they were all in there, growing ever more tired.

His wife met him at the door to their shared apartment as was routine; knowing his schedule intimately, she could rise to approach the door at the exact moment Patrick showed up at the other side. He entered and looked at her with his usual smile, which was, in every real way, a sincere one. She showed no signs of sinister cysts.

"How was your day?" she asked.

"Usual. You know. Typical," Patrick lied. All things considered, the whiteness of this lie paled bleached blank to his other transgression.

"That's good, Sweetheart. You ready?"

"Yes."

She looked the sort of beautiful-exhausted of mothers of two-month-olds: the fear on her face in recognition of the freedom she'd lost for good mixed with the novel love for another human she never knew existed, as if the love was hiding in some shadowy place, waiting for her to give birth so it could spring. The last nine hours of her life were spent pacing and feeding their child, and it was understood that when Patrick returned from work, he would take the child and begin the laborious process of putting him to sleep. Already spent, Patrick obliged nightly with a happy heart; to sooth a child into sleep is a magic proving over and over again to the secular world that it exists.

The child was affixed to his wife's breast and when she removed him in order to hand him over, Patrick looked at it, exposed inelegantly from the stretched, pulled-down collar of her shirt. He took the child.

"I just want my body back," his wife said, covering, and walked over to the sofa where she slumped and was already nearly asleep. Aside from the comment, everything was going exactly according to plan, to schedule, to expectation. Except that, he *knew* his wife's name but felt he couldn't think it, as if it resisted his knowing despite his knowing.

"But look how big he's getting," Patrick said to her half-conscious form. "How healthy." He was reduced in her opinion, at least in that he was no longer central to her life. There wasn't the romantic, sexual love that attracted them originally, but a domestic love, something like appreciation for the way in which they so tenderly acclimated to servitude in two months. He felt as if he were becoming less substantial, less solid—phantasmal against the boldness of baby. She was different, a wholly new class of woman. Almost un-woman. For Patrick, it was as if she was a mother and not a woman, but it didn't bother him inasmuch as someone needed to be present to take care of their son, to raise him to be a good man, and doubtful of his own ability to meet the challenge, he valued her in the way one loves a precious thing they've bought but like to keep hidden away.

He cursed himself. He cursed the thoughts that came to him without his control. He cursed the monotheistic absurdity of monogamy. He cursed the knowledge that he didn't deserve his wife, that he was a man, bound to impulses against which he felt relentlessly vulnerable. Patrick cursed the very sky that beget him to air—kicked him from nest and gave him wings but no compass, gave him the instinct to kill but no skill for mercy. He cursed the truth: that he was what they warned you about; he was a man. Let loose. Always hunting.

To put him to sleep, Patrick would remove his shirt and cradle his son skin-to-skin while pacing the upstairs hallway, waiting as the cries of the boy became the coos of sleep became the drowsy insentience of infant rest. Each evening, he'd mumble something different, some mantra, to ease the boy away from the world. Tonight: "Just let the day go. Just let the day go." There was a song to it, a melody, an inflection as the words reached toward period. "Just let the day go." He moaned the song in decreasing volume with each repetition, in time to the boy's receding, and took in his entire form: the translucent eyelids, lined red at the base of the oddly long lashes; the hair darker around the ridge and back of the head as if already in the most advanced stages of male-pattern baldness; the tiny hands and impossibly small fingernails. All of the forces beyond his body that would act upon it all of his life like pressure on a submerged object. They surround us like water and I have no way of knowing how to buoy him to free air, he thought.

"Just let the day go."

And Patrick "Hawk" Awkly looked on in terror as his son's fingers, with their impossible nails, grabbed at his naked chest.

Flowers for Tikkun Olam

for Roberta Markovitz

<u>1</u>

God Constricts

"They have me walking around, eh, with no clothes on."

"They what now, Bubby?"

"They want to kill me. There's a buzzing in my room. Nurse! NURSE!"

"Bubby. Hey, Bub. Listen. Are you talking to a nurse?"

"Eh. What? There's a buzzing. Nurse, there's a buzzing. When are you going to come to Florida?"

"There, well. You know, Bub…soon. I can make it soon. What about Zayda? I hear he comes to see you every day."

"Oh. Don't let him fool you. He goes to the gym; he comes for five minutes. So he can say, eh, that he came here. Fools everybody. That fucker."

"Bubby, but your health. How's your health?" Seymour looked over at his wife, who forked petite bites of breakfast into her mouth. She glanced up with the all-too frank sympathy of a social worker: a quality for which he didn't question the authenticity but that frustrated him nevertheless. He'd been, always—from childhood, the womb—antagonistic to compassion. Loving to be touched, he squirmed when it was in reaction to his hurt. Seymour nodded her away. "Bubby, your health?"

"He cheated on me, eh, he always cheated on me. Now, eh, you know, sometimes you just want to give the whole damn thing up."

"But they help you walk around right, Bub? That's got to be good for you. Getting exercise. You know, moving around."

"And he shut down my bank accounts. I don't even, eh, have any money. And your father doesn't come down to see me. And your aunt is *his* daughter."

"Zayda's?"

"Eh, yeah. But I have the condo paid for. And there's nothing that can take that. Eh, there's a *buzzing*. I need to get a lawyer."

"A lawyer?"

Seymour's wife looked up at the suggestion, at the one-half of the conversation she could hear while he spoke into the phone. She mouthed the word *lawyer* with question-mark eyebrows and he shrugged question-mark shoulders.

"Eh. I'm going to sue the fucker."

"Bubby, but what about your health?"

"I, eh, always thought I was poor. When I saw the back accounts, I almost died."

"Bubby, okay. I'm going to come to Florida soon. But can you promise me one thing? Promise me you'll take the medicine they give you and you'll do what the doctors say. If they ask you to walk around, I think it's best if you do it."

"Sometimes, I just want to give the whole thing up."

"Bubs, you remember when I was down there before? You went around telling all your friends by the pool how handsome I was? Remember that?"

"Eh, now you're married." She laughed troubled into the receiver.

"So were all of their daughters."

She laughed again. It was the sort of peace for which the infrequency denoted a seeming fabrication.

"Seymour, I'm going to die soon."

"Bub."

"Eh, I'm going to die. But whenever there isn't enough room, you have to breathe in, to make room. When you're, eh, you're all there is, and you're taking up all the space, you have to breathe in. Like you're sucking in your stomach. And then, there's space to fill. So I'm gonna suck in soon. Make, eh, space."

Rather than redirect, Seymour decided to challenge the comment, as if a dedication to logic could (ever) push through disease, "What space, Bub? What's the space for, anyway?"

"Light, Seymour. Flowers."

Seymour looked over at his wife, whose eyes, down to not offend, typically trained upon that which needed the most attention. And because of it, because there were such staples, such buttresses of sturdiness in tumult, he could outlast just about anything (such conversations), whether he wanted to admit it or not.

Divine Light

The photocopied listing—complete with darkened pictures so heavily reproduced that the living room looked like the inside of a chimney—that the agent had handed Seymour told of 900 some-odd square feet and, admitting it was Philadelphia and they were already on a tight leash for what they could afford, he scoffed at the closet of a house, "My bookshelves to the roof." But when Maggie fell in love with it, he borrowed from the bank and began the arduous process of moving furniture through doors not built for people with furniture. He had to saw the queen box-spring in half only to sister the destroyed joints with 2 X 2 lumber in the bedroom the bed would ubiquitously fill; they had to jump over the foot-board to alight upon their reserved sleeping sides. She loved the small house so much that he accepted it too, loving it because he loved her in it. He even ignored the slight bowing of the ceiling bordering the two floors: Home Inspector, "All the houses this old, around here, do that." What he at first pictured for himself—a large, spacious home, well-lit by a profusion of windows, with enough rooms for him to study, exercise, sleep, cook—ceded calmly into an appreciation for the tiny row home on the blue-collar block. Its size contained them, hugged them close together with its walls, so that they were never far apart. A large suburban home, conversely, with its second floor all but ignored and avoided, would emphasize (demand!) their separateness: the echoes of their voices finding one another far too late. The small house, then, worked well to emphasize the first years of Seymour and Maggie's marriage.

And his bookshelves fit in the room they used for an office just fine.

Seymour and Maggie filled it with light.

He replaced all of the insane blue fluorescent bulbs of the previous owner with the warm shine of faux-day. If this was the vessel that was to chart their voyage through early love, as they found their marital sea legs (if you'll permit it), it would have to be warmly lit with the primordial quality of day, even at night. So he carefully twisted in all of the new bulbs and flicked the switches.

<u>3</u>

Filling the Vessels

In ten years, Seymour and Maggie added the complements and accouterments that made the same house seem new. Window boxes. A patio table. LED strip lighting under the cabinets. Shutters carefully painted with the color scheme of the front door. A garden. These were the things homeowners did to turn one's fidelity to a fine geographic point into the vestiges of nuance. It was no different than buying many hats for the same head.

But Seymour, ever the progressive-minded anti-capitalist (he was an English professor; we must forgive) felt an acute discomfort in the accumulation of *things*. Not an outright frustration for the American tenets of materialism (though he used this exact expression one evening at a bar with friends, the idiosyncratic proselytizing of the first pint becoming the near-quarrel of *ad nauseam* ennui by pint four) but more so a strange and core-oriented feeling of guilt. Being white, straight, and male, he had only his Jewishness and working class upbringing on which to hang his disposition toward identifying as marginalized. (Contemporary Literary Theory had taunted him). He knew it was a sham, but felt he had to flex his faux-marginalization during faculty holiday parties where the increasingly young new-hires (pre-tenure, and so, tenuous) jockeyed for esoteric esteem by quoting the latest article in Queer Theory or Post-Colonialism as if they'd written it themselves, or as if they were ready to judge a stationed Full Professor as a hegemonic charlatan if he (surely, a he) had not himself read it. Seymour once wore a yarmulke to a Christmas party and refused to stand near the Nativity; later, this made him feel like a bad person, or at least he suspected others might think of him as a bad person if they knew his true intentions (to fit in as an outsider) so he promised himself to never do such a thing again. He failed, because everyone fails at virtue. He wasn't a bad person, though the Jewishness of his family ended, really, with his Bubby. (The yarmulke was cut from a knit cap).

However, Seymour did grow up in near poverty. His parents divorced when he was young and his mother, caring for him and his brother, worked two jobs in order to support the small family. She was so often at work that his childhood memories were nearly bereft of her completely. They lived in a Jewish part of Philadelphia, along a long row of storefronts selling varieties of fabrics until Fourth Street hit Washington Avenue, where tenement towers rose as if giant forbears. He was forbidden to walk south of their apartment, to get within the shadows falling from the towers, to even admit that the monoliths existed. And despite the threadbare upholstery of the sofa that came with the rent, or the blandness of their hotplate meals, Seymour never knew he was poor. His mother made sure not to use the word, to never complain about money, to treat her children to the small meaningful things that accounted for the very last of her earnings; when the time came, she paid for his college, entirely.

Years later, the local synagogue would be converted to luxury condos, the Stars of David scratched from the sandstone façade.

These things, only retrospectively, caused the guilt Seymour felt when his mother (now alone, now lonely) spoke of avoiding the holidays ("My fingers, the joints, I can't bake.") or when his Bubby called from the hospital in Florida, where her dementia took her past and present ("When will you come?").

At the faculty parties, however, he never flouted his previous poverty, never turned out his empty pockets for the affectation of Marxist sentimentality, and so it was his Jewishness that won the day. The mockery of poorness too much touched the guilt he had for leaving poverty behind through no definitive work of his own.

Added to these guilt-addled cogitations—and perhaps thrusting them—was Seymour's irrepressible displeasure in being born. That isn't to say he suffered from existential anxiety wrought from questions of self-value or even embedded depression; rather, his perturbation's trail-head was situated in the labor he had caused his mother: both in birthing and rearing him. He hated to think that most of his human life, until about the age where he was capable of self-sufficiency (when was this? after college? at tenure?), was spent in dependence of someone else's sweetness. His mother fed him. Clothed him. Roused him at the waking hour to be whisked away by buses to drab schools. Because of her love, her disposition toward love, he was able to survive—thrive. And *only* because of that, the roll of the dice that is being born in the first place, could he become himself. And now, a fully grown (really, he was short) man, he hadn't the slightest idea at how to repay the debt. The quickening of this guilt caused him much pain in college and continued with inertia and exponent integers until the present date.

How to repay the Universe for its roulette.

Do the same for a new generation?

This prompted, of course, the question of progeny, to which his potential dedication went, when Maggie quasi-queried, like this:

"Your mother called again. Is still asking."

"Asking?"

"You know," Maggie said, watching for the facial inflections that indicated either amusement or a rapidly progressing frustration-to-anger, "Children."

"Ah, yes. Reproduction. The bodily-hardwired urge of ego-centrism."

"Is that a quote?"

"Of mine."

"Then, Seymour, I think you should be a writer."

"I'm rotten enough at teaching the stuff. Can't imagine I'd want to poison the well by pissing myself into it."

"I'm running out of things to tell her."

Conversations like this occurred only and often at the dinner table. It was the repository for spousal conversation wherein two people, at the end of their days, found one another again in an agreed-upon spot, the place of common refuge. The dinner table, where the coals could be turned over and the batter could be smoothed in the low heat of the furnace below. The previous ten years of Seymour and Maggie's marriage was not the triviality one might glean from their dinner-table conversations. Together, they had traveled the world, not as tourists but as hikers, tent-campers. They backpacked Machu Picchu and irrigated farmland on the Ethiopian/Eritrean frontier. Seymour took an idiosyncratic interest in translating lost teenage Salvadorian poets, and so traveled to Santiago de Maria, El Salvador on a leave-of-absence from his university, to claim relics estranged even from the big online book seller (you know the one). While there, Maggie attempted to develop support infrastructure for gay Salvadorian men often ostracized to the point of murder (a beheading, when they were there) in the small, mainly Christian (WWJD?) *pueblitos*. And so on. They did it all rarely staying in a hotel. Hostels, makeshift B&Bs, tents; they had put good use to their decade, dedicating it to the expansion of their minds, and to each other. So it was upon this that Seymour landed on the tired reply:

"Tell her we've got too much to do. You know, for ourselves. I've got to publish something practically every semester if I want

70

promotion, and I don't think they'll be buying Spanish poetry much longer. And we're too selfish, in the sense that we like traveling too much, spending too much on downtown dinners, reading in a quiet peace, to raise children. It wouldn't be fair to them. But you know, maybe one day; we can always adopt. Right?"

"But she's *your* mother, Seymour. You tell her."

"Wait! Mag, you're with me on this, right?"

She was, "I am. Though sometimes—and this isn't some womanly mother-instinct that you're armed to levy; I see your eyes—sometimes I can't help but feel that when people say parenthood is the most amazing thing a person can experience, they're telling the truth. And look at us, faithful to experience as if our sole worth will be added up upon arrival to Heaven—" Seymour coughed—"in some celestial bank account of a life-well-lived. I just can't help feeling that we're almost hypocritical in potentially missing out on what is understood to be the most fulfilling of human experiences."

"So," Seymour responded, wine flushing his cheeks and causing his eyes to follow her neckline, plunging, "you're saying that you want to do this as a selfish experiment?"

"Not that I want to. But that if I did, it would be for that. For selfishness. Yes. Right."

"That's something I can get behind," he said, actually getting up to get behind her. He encompassed her shoulders with his arms—her favorite thing—and held fast. He moved the hair from her cheek with his nose and kissed the revealed spot. "I'll call my mother in the morning, tell her to leave your womb alone."

He didn't.

4

Delivering the Vessels

Populating houses is like having children, and this is how: both are things that contain things. Vessels that are vehicles. Houses contain lives, the bodies and effects of the people they habituate. The Philadelphia row homes, with their long, connected, brick façades, separating neighbors only by shared walls—never nearly soundproofed enough—were built for utility: a young overpopulated city, not enough space, density, etc. 20th Century working men could walk from their small homes to large factories in neighborhoods built around factories: shad fisheries and baseball manufacturers, rope makers for seafarers and bottlers for cola companies. Now every warehouse had been converted into artist studios with first-floor steakhouses charging $70 for organic free-range Wagyu cuts and the cloistered homes surrounding them were considered cute. But what houses were really for were to contain the family. Their walls—brick or stucco or linoleum or steel or clay—protected that which was inside and did so against all the weather beyond.

And children, similarly, contain the whispers of their parents, the traces of spirit and gene that are the closet hopes of immortality for perpetually dying carbon-based organisms. Bearing children: a big *whew*, I can die now, because I'll still be here. Seymour never used this expression, though he wanted to, at coed baby showers, to take a little brilliance out of the sheen. Every impending father looked as if he had an upset stomach.

But secretly, at least unconsciously, Seymour delighted in thinking a little Maggie might run around the Earth. The conceit of it, the spoil, was that she wouldn't *be* Maggie. She'd be an "individual." She could grow up to be a Republican, marry a Republican. She could believe in the 2nd Amendment. She could believe in female subservience, that institutionalized racism was somehow biologically justified. That all of her birthrights were actually rights by birth. God, the horror! Yahweh! That his cherished, adorable daughter could grow to be a little shit was enough a temporary justification for his vasectomy ("We're sure this can be reversed, Doctor?" "In most cases, yes. But it's best to acknowledge that this may be permanent." "Fine fine. Snip it. There's always adoption.").

The difference is that homes are sedentary vessels while children are vessels sent out unto the Earth, fragile as soon as they are placed down. What they contain can be spilled at the smallest tip, through the smallest crack. No matter what a parent does, all he puts in a child can be spoiled at the moment he sends the vessel into the world. So it was this element of his posthumous existence, smuggled into the nest of a body Maggie and he could form, that was no surer than his darker ruminations about his own self-worth. Who read his translations? What did his students really learn? Why eat right? Why reattach his vasa deferentia?

Seymour wondered if the vessel that *he* was, sent from *his* parents and containing the light that *they* were, was what they'd wanted to give the world. Was he sound?, intact and sealed with their souls? Or had he cracked, fallen, let loose their best efforts? He felt, in his everyday affairs, that there was a constant need to substantiate himself as the vessel for those who begot him. He held his abdominal muscles taut (they were there, under the cushion of his forties) as if to keep in their light. His mother's, really.

"Are you thinking about yourself as a vessel again?" Maggie asked in the dark. He wished he'd not revealed this line of thinking to her after an evening of spirits: fluid, not spectral. His translated manuscript, *El Jibarito*, by a Puerto Rican farmer, had been rejected, again.

"How did you know?"

"You're on your back, staring at the ceiling." He slept only on his sides.

"How can you tell what I'm looking at? It's dark."

"There's nothing else up there."

"Maybe I need to go downstairs, watch TV or something."

"You're not a vessel. Or, if you are, that's not all you are."

"Can I turn on the hall light? I don't like to step where the house bows."

"I know, go ahead. But, Seymour, really, you should relax. You're not this thing holding your mother. You kill yourself with this idea that you're letting her down. You're a professor. You're a good husband. You speak two languages."

"Maybe I should learn another."

"Maybe you should kiss your wife."

"You're a good wife," he leaned over to kiss her. He missed her mouth, aimed again, missed it. Found it.

"You just need to know that I love you. That's it. You don't need to contain anything. And you don't need to turn the light on; you know exactly where the house bows."

"I know, Mag. All of the above. I know."

<u>5</u>

The Shattering of the Vessels

That Maggie *could* have an affair negated for Seymour any realistic belief that she actually would. Suddenly, the bricks aggregating to form the fronts of Philadelphia houses showed their cement seams. If you ran your finger along the line, the grey dust residue of the mortar would release itself upon your finger suggesting that if you rubbed long enough, you'd get between the bricks; you'd be able to topple the whole damn thing. The lamplight inside could squeak out. Her admission of the affair was instant, and Seymour's subsequent inquiry—not to last less than perhaps forever—was comprehensive. Maggie answered every question in stride, her pain leavened with a pride derived from the knowledge that the isolated incident's exclusivity was punctuated with the hardest stop grammar could muster. Surely Seymour could understand the metaphor. She was contrite. Conciliatory. Repentant. Penitent. A thesaurus full of sorry. But she answered every question he asked (would probably continue to answer questions long after Seymour had forgiven her and they went to live on as happily ever after as the medieval adage would allow) because she was focused solely on one thing: the next ten years. The ten after that. Her repairing the shards of her fractured home. And she, the hammer holder.

He started with the most prosaic questions:

Who? "*Mark, from work.*"

What? "*Sex. Penetration.*"

When? "*After a happy hour. You were at a conference giving the paper on Romance Language Acquisition and the Pedagogical Function of Intra-Lingual Colloquial Aesthetics.*"

Where? "*A hotel.*"

How? "*I was terribly drunk, so I couldn't think.*" Not that How; How? "*Really?*" How? "*Mostly him on top.*" Mostly? "*And a little, me.*"

The primordial, Why? "*I don't know.*" You must. "*No.*" You must. "*No.*" Ad infinitum.

Which ceded, per sequitur, into the complex questions:

How could you? "*There's no logic to it, it was an accident.*"

Like a car crash? "*Like black ice.*"

What if I go do it? There's a student, very beautiful, chews a pen while looking at me… "*I suppose I'd deserve that.*"

How could you do this to us? "*It was easier than I expected, so I wasn't as careful as I should have been.*"

Easier? "*I never, not in a million years, considered that I would do that. So, I guess, I was vulnerable to doing it.*"

Did you like it? "*Seymour.*"

Did you? "*I hated it.*"

Is that a lie? "*I wouldn't start now.*"

Maggie had married Seymour because she was desperate to lead the prescribed life of the women in her family; but unlike them—in the way that arranged marriages often promoted a love between the couple—Maggie grew to love Seymour in a completely undefinable fashion. What started antithetical to a love story (he was mired in graduate work, stoop-backed with the albatross of his own expectation; she obsessed with domesticity: creating culinary masterworks that ended with overly salted/bittered/spiced concoctions resulting in Chinese takeaway or pizza-by-the-slice from the corner store) grew into a partnership wherein the two of them were independent of each other while seemingly in league with the same scheme. It was as if being in the traditionally subjugate paradigm of matrimony provided her with the agency to develop herself against its most strident precepts. She even went to college. Maggie hadn't nearly hoped to find this sort of companionship in a spouse, so she married Seymour on the pretense that he was handsome and kosher (he was playing that card even in graduate school), but soon found him to exceed her greatest expectations. Plainly, he was a man. He was in no way grandiose or perfect or wild or exceptional. What she had always assumed a husband would be—an icon of masculinity steadfast against the inertia of a spinning Earth—was replaced in Seymour with what he truly was: a very common, very lovable, thing.

So when Maggie had her affair, it was almost as shocking to her as it was calculated. Because everyone knows when they're about to have an affair. Perhaps just a bit disingenuous in answering Seymour's queries, Maggie was not ignorant to the flirtations, the innuendos, Mark's hand brushing. She knew very well what was happening, but she was so obstinate to the potential that, as it was happening—literally, the moment when Mark moved inside of her—she was more curious than anything. It wasn't until afterwards, furiously washing him out of her in the hotel bathroom, that the shock began to wear off and the bricks of her home began to tremble in earnest.

In the following weeks, Maggie and Seymour were very careful with one another. Seymour couldn't believe how quickly he had forgiven her. Of course he didn't tell her this. Of course he went to bars, plotting his revenge, finding out just how difficult (impossible) it was to actually lure a woman away for sex. Of course it pained him to look at her, to watch her figure wrapped in a robe after exiting the shower, to know another man had been with that body—*in* that body. He objectified her like that, her body—*his* body—at the disposal of someone else, despite promises and vows and the abbreviations of animal lust reeling against the arrogance of structured monogamy. It pained him to see her sitting with coffee on the sofa; perhaps he looked at her more now, more when she wasn't noticing, more when he could see her as she was, apart from him. He hated to think of his new status: cuckold; the Shakespearean archaism that would have to end in a high-noon pistol-duel but would really just recede into nothing, his cuckolder riding safely off into the sunset with no bullets in his body by high-one, high-two, high-three...

Seymour demanded that Maggie quit her job. She refused. He dropped it.

That house of theirs became for Seymour the biggest thing in the world. The square-footage, so scant before, tripled—quadrupled, quintupled—each day as Seymour understood more and more how important it was to him. He knew that Maggie and he would survive it; he'd read Updike, he'd read essentially every American master of the twentieth century (well, yes, the men); he knew how common infidelity was in marriage. But he figured it would have been him. Perhaps it was unrealistic in the first place, regardless of the fact that he had never—would never (oh, who knows, maybe)—do it himself. So he ultimately knew that they would be able to move beyond this particular tribulation into what they once were, or at least get close to it. Maggie's guilt seemed even more than that which he felt for abandoning his mother; in some sense it actually rescinded that guilt, alleviating Seymour from the stress of his own preoccupations.

They made love again not long after, but not quickly either. Not quickly in the sense that it wasn't too near Maggie's indiscretion, nor not quickly in the sense that the love-making was slow, in the physical—i.e. Department of Physics—sense. They did not discuss it. They did not exchange the rather formal knowing glances. They did not prepare in the usual way: pre-coital lubricants, coital props, post-coital towels; arranged politely on a bedside table. Separate bathroom visits; phones on silent. They didn't even attempt foreplay. When evening came, they went up into the darkness and got under the blankets. They set alarm clocks. They exhaled the final deep breaths of the day, and Seymour rolled toward and on top of Maggie, where she accepted him and they very quietly re-consummated their union. It was the sort of love-making where both had their hands on each other's faces.

The next evening, at dinner, the phone rang and, despite the normal prohibition restricting outside interlocution while at the table, Maggie felt a renewed stability in her marriage that allowed for her answering it.

"It's for you, Seymour. I think it's your Bubby."

6

Tikkun Olam

The first thing Seymour noticed was that "Delray Beach" was a close translation of "the King's beach" and that this was just north of "Boca Ratón": a close translation of the "mouse's mouth." Also, that "Florida" was a close translation of "flowery." So that together, at the front door of the Florida Boca Ratón Delray Florist (see: Flowery mouse mouth of the King's beach florist) he nearly condemned bilingualism altogether.

The Jewish New Yorkers and Philadelphians, who had worked their long lives to the quick, bought up condo real estate on coastal Florida almost as if by instinct, just as they felt the telltale signs of decomposition in their worn joints. It was as if they had an irresistible urge to sit around a communal pool in visors and too-revealing swim wear (grey chest hair; purple varicose veins) to talk about the attractiveness of their respective grandchildren, the *schvartzes* of Miami, the *feygelas* of Key West. They brought *the north* with them, opening cheese-steak and bagel shops (various smears) and dotting the east-west highways that fed the ocean to the marsh swamps of central Florida with synagogues in juxtaposition to the palm trees. Bubbies and Zaydas in the thousands came to Florida for the sun and promptly fired up their air conditioners. People drove slowly and everyone seemed to be angry. They all thought everything their grandchildren did was *mishuga*, regardless of their beauty.

The florist's impartial smile was as tranquilizing as it was disconcerting. Every time Seymour attempted small-talk while the man carefully arranged the purchased flowers in the vase, the man simply smiled a bit more profoundly, not answering but somehow managing to not be rude either. There was a trained docility to the man: the way he arranged each stem as if by ikebana, the tenderness with which he seemed to coax the petals from their bulbs, stroking them on the underside like under a child's chin. He looked at Seymour with politeness each time Seymour forced one of the awkward extrapolations in an effort to thwart the silence Americans uniquely considered uncomfortable ("Hot in Florida, yeah?"; "Mouse's mouth, right?"); but the florist's main focus was always the flowers. He handled them as if he were handling the divine. Seymour came in with a "you choose" attitude, and said as much to the florist, who began designing the vase of flowers with artistic license. The motley scents matched the colors. The arrangement, Seymour began to see, had an intention to it that was near brilliant, almost sublime. He couldn't look at it for fear of blindness and he couldn't turn away for fear of regret. The florist's hands moved around the flowers, and without feeling the accompanying emotion for the action, Seymour noticed himself to be crying. He saw the curves of his wife in the stems, smelled the scent of Maggie in the fragrance—under the perfume, that which was *her* scent. He knew the petal-softness as the down on her cheek and found the correlation so apt that he simply shook his head at it. There too, in the flowers, was his mother. She also grew delicately from the ground and had, in her, sweet breath: a nest for bees, stingers retracted, protected in the euphoria of intoxication. Seymour even saw himself, there, in the bundle. His face in the ovaries. His sinews in stem. They were all there, in the vase.

"I'm sorry," he said. "I don't know what's come over me. I'm not really even sentimental. I…"

The florist, noticing Seymour and his tears, instantly stopped arranging the flowers. He seemed to know he'd reached the desired effect, and so he lifted the vase carefully and handed it across the counter to Seymour, still saying nothing. Seymour took the vase. "Thank you; they're lovely." And the strangest, seemingly most random thought occurred to him: the cool porcelain of the vase, its smooth curve, reminded him of a child. He knew this didn't make sense, children were warm and curved quite differently, but he thought it nevertheless. A new human. Something he and Maggie might do, might make.

He paid, thanking the florist again, and left.

The Delray Medical Center was as garish an edifice as anything Seymour had seen in South Florida; its hotel-box-like architecture was saved from the Art Deco pastels of Miami by protractor right angles and the beigest of sandstone stucco. Florida seemed to take its inspiration from the brown boxes of delivery services, only painted with the colors left for the Pasch holidays when artists from everywhere else bought out the rest of the spectrum. South Florida looked like a collection of square Easter eggs.

When Seymour stepped into his Bubby's room, the first thing he noticed was the buzzing.

"Eh, Seymour!"

"Hi, Bub."

"Eh, aren't you handsome? You get that from your mother's side. How's Amy?"

"Maggie."

"Maggie."

"She's good, Bub. Sends her love. She doesn't have the time off that I get."

"When are you going to get a job at PENN?"

"Someday, Bub. Someday. So how are you anyway?"

Seymour hadn't moved more than a few steps into the room. Though his Bubby's bed was close by, he had trouble approaching it. The way she looked, cloistered in the sterility of the room's whiteness, pushed at the bruise of his guilt.

"Did I ever tell you, you were named for my brother? He died of brain cancer."

She'd told him this, "You've told me this. His name was Scott." This was an old game.

"And you're Seymour. Eh, S just like the S in Scott. And you're such a handsome boy. From your mother's side. Surely not from old Bubby's side."

"Oh, Bub."

"Eh, come here already."

And Seymour did. But his legs were unsure, his steps timid, which resulted in his totter, a stumble, and his fling forward. The vase ascended from his hand in a hostile parabola and fell upon the room's tiles, shattering the porcelain to the furthest reaches of the room, and spreading the flowers out, sopped as they were in their own water, in a fanned crown.

Seymour, shocked on the floor, watched as his Bubby got up, came around the bed, and stooped with great care to lift each flower from the floor. "They're beautiful, Seymour, really. Eh, shards of light. Let's pick them up together."

El Trauma de Claudia

To leave the San Salvador airport, William Sterling had to press a button that triggered one of three bulbs in the stoplight at the customs desk to randomly illuminate. The green *pase* light flashed briefly and the customs guard nodded at him, pointing over his shoulder toward the exit. Sterling picked up his duffel and proceeded out.

It was December, and the Central American heat was different from the desert heat he was used to; it was more fragrant, oddly floral. Around him, families hugged at length and spoke in raised, rapid voices to loved ones home from other countries, the US mostly, with take-away McDonald's *Happy Meals* on ice and *I ♥NY* t-shirts in a variety of sizes. Although obviously among the only *extranjeros* present, no one paid him much mind other than a dark and wrinkled-skinned man selling postcards and a police officer, who held a polished silver shotgun and looked at Sterling's tidy beige uniform intently.

"The bus to San Salvador?" he asked the officer. Sterling's passable Spanish—learned from lisping Barcelonan high school teachers and weekend trips to Mexico—would finally be tested.

"It departs on the hour, there," the officer said, pointing to a nearby concrete platform. "You are American of the military, yes?"

"Not right now. And not for the following two weeks."

"You speak well."

"And you equally."

The officer laughed. "Do you come from war?"

"Listen, how long until the following bus?"

"Less than half hour, sir. Welcome. And why do you arrive in El Salvador?"

"I don't know how it is said in Spanish," Sterling replied. "In English, it is called 'surfing.' Upon the waves."

"Yes," the officer said. "The same. La Libertad is famous for tourists. But look, now arrives your bus early."

"Thank you," Sterling said, turning to go.

"Good," replied the officer.

The bus was overcrowded but a certain reverence of space for the tall foreigner provided Sterling with a seat and room for his duffel. He did not want special treatment, but wanted even less to explain why.

He wanted two things only during his leave: solitude and the ocean.

The bus rode along the highway past roadside stands selling fruit and *horchata*. Occasionally, men would jog along the briefly slowing bus and jump upon the running board, grabbing onto rails attached to the side. In the distance, Sterling could see wide-reaching mountain ranges, their peaks scattered but beautiful. He stared at them until dust from the road tickled his eyes closed. He'd heard of the Salvadorian beaches—their warm waters curled like the tips of flame in perfect tunnels to glide through—from a private in his company, a man from Sonsonate, in the *Occidente* of El Salvador.

"Cincinnati?" Sterling had asked, in response to the private naming his hometown.

"*Son-so-na-te*," the private repeated, with emphasis.

"You're saying Cincinnati," Sterling said, his mouth a wry smile. "You must be from Ohio."

"Whore mother," the private said, in Spanish. "You would be lucky to be from such a place as I."

"Do not be preoccupied," Sterling said.

The private laughed, "You will like the *señoritas*, too."

But that was back in the desert. The private had told Sterling of the ocean, the waves, the women; but he never mentioned the mountains. These kept Sterling's attention as the bus went on. He longed to climb them, to find their peaks and see what vantages they presented. There, at the highest point of the country, he could breathe thin air and watch the ocean for miles, until he could imagine the waters falling from the long defunct theory of the edge of the world.

The bus slowed as it approached the border of San Salvador. Ahead, Sterling could see a dog, dead, on the road. By its side was another dog, dirty and apparently homeless, of another breed, but resting its head on the snout of its fallen comrade either in a sad act of compassion or perhaps tragic personal loss. As the bus picked up again and passed the dogs, one of the young men hanging from a rail yelled *chucha*, and delivered a kick to the living dog's side, the bus's velocity aiding to the ferocity of the strike. Sterling turned with the feeling of wanting to look away from something because it hurts the heart too much. This was not the peak of a distant mountain. It was not the lonely lolling of the ocean.

He had arrived in San Salvador.

* * *

A *boracho* stumbled through an intersection and between a line of stopped cars with a half-empty bottle of foreign Vodka, pleading lackadaisically with bloodshot eyes and a wavering cupped hand to drivers for alms. Sterling looked only long enough to wonder at the series of cars that obliged. Silver US currency exchanged from the hand of each driver to that of the wayward man; US money that, by way of some distant war and even more distant politics, had become the national currency of this Central American country.

He turned around and faced the dim-lit far wall of his hotel room. It was windowless and soot-blacked with dirt. On the single bed against the wall lay his duffel; he hadn't bothered to open it since taking it from the carousel at the airport. Inside were only the most sentimental things he couldn't live without while away from home, anyway. They were inessential things, but his drill sergeant said he'd need inessential things the most while on tour: photos, a bathing suit, hair gel—the latter unusable with his sickled scalp but brought along for the familiar smell. Home, he'd apply it to his shoulder-length blond hair after coming out of the water, a trick to tease the girls in the suggestion that his hair was naturally swept back by the tenderness of the ocean. Sterling sat on the bed, noticing one of the legs at the foot was short, which caused him to lean forward, and brought his hand backward over his rough head.

The familiar ache in his left knee stabbed again. He pressed his thumb deep into the pain, the dull bruising force alleviating the sharp insistence deep inside the joint.

The room was otherwise empty.

There was a rumor that central San Salvador was dangerous for foreigners. It was why the best restaurants had armed guards, why the police were military. But Sterling had to get out.

He walked from his hotel to the Catedral de San Salvador. Unlike his dark room, the Catedral was as regal as any he'd seen before. The vaulted nave's pink and green stained glass windows augmented the passing light and left patches of color on Sterling's forearms as he knelt forward and rested them on the pew in front of him. He wanted to pray. A part of him needed to pray. But it was as if he'd forgotten how. He thought the word *God*, but it was uninspired, abstract. As a boy, he could always at least envision an old man, Michelangelo's Sistine impression of divinity. Here, there was nothing. He thought the word *Dios* but the net gain was the same. There were names he'd have to pray for. Men in the desert; men whose idle time was bookended by loud quick rushes of wind and movement. But he'd forgotten them. He couldn't remember the name of the private from Sonsonate. He'd forgotten the *Creeds*, the *Lord's Prayer*; all that was left was to move his arms back and forth slowly, to watch the colored patches fall from his skin to the wood of the pew.

"That's enough, Old Boy," he thought to himself. "It's called *leave* because it means *permission*. It's a permission to forget it all for a second."

So Sterling genuflected, crossing himself as he had after scoring a base hit while playing high school baseball, as he did before leaving his quarters in the desert, and got up to go.

Outside, a short man in a button-down shirt—with only two buttons from the bottom, buttoned up—approached Sterling. "Monseñor Romero is open for five minutes more."

"What?"

"The crypt, still it is open. Will you come?"

Sterling followed the man to the door that led down into the crypt. There, with four bronze nuns sentry like bedposts at the corners of his tomb, lay the remains of Oscar Romero, interred in the marble of the floor. Upon the prostrate statue's fissured chest rested a polished red sphere, an abstract indication of where his assassin's bullet found the Holy Man's heart.

The man who showed him down into the crypt gesticulated excitedly, leading Sterling around the adjacent rooms with the expedition of a tour guide who had only a few moments before the tour was over and the tip depended on the authenticity of the exhibition. Sterling gave him whatever paper was in his pocket to send him away. Without a word, the man went.

Sterling walked back to Romero, now alone, and considered the memorial. The red sphere caught candlelight. He leaned in and looked closer, squinting. The sphere seemed to move deeper into the bronze chest of the Monseñor.

"It is time now, we go," said the man in struggling English, who had returned and touched Sterling gently on the shoulder, to raise him from his reverie.

"That was a long five minutes," Sterling replied.

"I am sorry, Señor, but I do not speak English," the man said.

"It is clear," said Sterling. "I had said nothing."

That was Sterling's one day in San Salvador, El Salvador.

Saint Savior, The Savior.

Because perhaps the small country offered some sort of salvation.

"You've arrived from Europe?" asked the man at the desk of the hotel in La Libertad. Sterling had left the bus moments before, using his hand to bridge the forehead over his eyes against the high sun to see the caress of blue-green water flop playfully against the sand. He had entered the hotel, which was markedly nicer than the one in the capitol—an effort to reserve splendor for tourists, surely. It was obvious: they were everywhere. La Libertad seemed to be where everyone who journeyed to El Salvador ended up. Something about it made Sterling feel fraudulent. He presumed that away upon the distant mountains, there weren't any such interlopers. Here, at the beaches, they alighted from airplanes in droves.

"Not Europe, but close," said Sterling.

"You are German?"

"Not close."

"Please, Señor, tell me? Americano?"

"Quite."

"It was the uniform that made me guess," the clerk said. "I know that all Germans wear them. You have the blond hair of Germany."

"I don't have any hair presently."

"But when you do it is the color of Germany."

"Perhaps it is in the blood of my grandfathers."

"That is a peculiar expression."

"I don't know the expressions of El Salvador."

"You will learn, señor. . ." The clerk looked down into a book opened on the desk in front of him.

"Sterling."

"Sterling. Clearly. But I do not see the name here."

"I haven't made a reservation. Is there habitation?"

"Of course. How many days will you stay?"

"I have two weeks."

"That will not be much time to learn expressions."

"I learn rapidly."

The man closed his book and moved over to the register. "I always thought Americanos were funny. I can understand English a little you know, when it is spoken slowly," he said, nodding at the television behind him, "and we get many dramas from the United States. Americanos are funny."

"Everyone's funny to everyone else."

"Yes, it is true. Then, will you stay the two weeks."

"What is your rate?"

"Reasonable."

"How many does it cost?" Sterling asked.

"Very cheap."

"And the ocean here is good? The waves?"

"Perfect."

"Good. I will take the habitation."

"I am Rogelio, señor Sterling, and I am here every day."

"Thank you, Rogelio."

"And to be less formal, you may call me Roge. I am grateful that you speak the proper tongue. Many tourists do not and we must speak with our hands. I know enough English to answer their questions, though. They always ask the same ones."

His room overlooked the beach. If he woke suddenly from sleep, confused about where he was, the view could easily trick him into thinking he was back home, looking at the Pacific from Southern California.

Men on long wooden boats with single motors ushered groups of tourists into the ocean, creating wake that rocked Sterling on his board. He lay face up, with his eyes closed, surrounded front and back with the most regal exhibits of nature. The ocean moved below him and the sun warmed from above; he lay still—while the best waves to ride rode under him—thinking about the Pacific. It was the same ocean, the same water from home, impossibly here, having traveled hundreds of miles. And there *he* was, similar, having traveled thousands: the same man, the same skin, in a new place with the same water. He couldn't fit it all together.

A man conducting one of the passing boats shouted, "Cuidate, el mar te llevará." *Be careful, the ocean will take you.* "Take me," he thought.

It was early; Sterling always preferred surfing in the morning, as close to sunrise as he could get it. That was when the ocean was most welcoming, when the others in the water were as passionate as he was. The early surfers would nod at each other, each aware of the passion it took to rise that early, with only subtle light, and meet the ocean; to play on it like children in the sand, without care or even recognition of its vastness or depth, or what hid below. That early in the morning, the ocean was innocuous, an enormous vault about which the surfers cared only for the gold gilding of the door. The curl of gravity and shore. But even as Sterling lay there, he could hear the others gathering at the cafés and beach houses that lined the sand. Even that early, the tourists had awakened.

He had maybe a half hour before they crowded the water, but he did not stand upon the board. He lay, eyes closed to the sun, chancing undertow.

The next morning Sterling asked Roge for a café good enough for locals.

He sat with a dark coffee on an outdoor porch facing the ocean. The morning was quiet, and now, three days into his leave, he began to relax into civilian life. He sipped the coffee slowly, leaned back upon the two posterior legs of his chair, and thumbed the pain in his knee.

"Hello, Sir. I am the waitress with your coffee. You would like another?"

"I can comprehend you," Sterling said, in her language. The girl was young with very long and very straight brown hair. He noticed it first because it was split in the back and brought forward upon each shoulder, down her front as if it shielded her from unwanted attention. She bore a subtle mole upon her lip, the color of her hair and eyes, and as she smiled, it lifted. She was partially backlit from the sun, so Sterling could not see her plainly. She noticed him squinting and so moved to the side.

"Very well," she said, now in full view. Sterling looked immediately down at his coffee, feeling somehow embarrassed, then developed the courage to look at her again. She spoke very rapidly then, and Sterling was unable to understand her. He felt embarrassed again, having just told her that he could speak her language and was presently exhibiting that he could not. Her face had commanded the concentration needed to translate. But days ago, he carried a heavy gun and a heavier burden to use it, so, he thought to himself, I can find the courage now.

He reached his hand forward and held her forearm. "More slowly, more slowly, please."

"Oh, I am sorry," she said. "I suppose I was excited. Though I want to practice my English."

"We can practice it."

"I wish to speak it one day."

"I wish to speak it with you."

She laughed calmly. "Well, I asked if I could get you more coffee and something to eat."

"Yes. More coffee. What have you to eat?"

"Most take *pupusas* for breakfast."

"Then I will take what most take."

"How many would you like?" she asked.

"How many for a man like me?"

"Possibly two."

"Then exactly two, please."

The waitress smiled and went away into the café. Sterling breathed deeply. This felt normal. Speaking with a young woman, a beautiful and kind woman, was normal. He felt charming again, something he hadn't felt for a long while. He felt the flirtatious echo of his past rise, welcome after the months of bravado that had made him hard.

She returned with the coffee and two overlapping tortillas.

"These are your *pupusas*?" Sterling asked.

"Inside, there is cheese and beans," the woman responded. "You can put this on top," she said, putting a bottle of red sauce on the table.

"What is your name?" Sterling asked.

The waitress attempted to control her smile, resulting in only the corners angling up, "I call myself Claudia."

"I call myself Billy."

"It is good to know you, Billy," Claudia said, reaching for his hand.

"Equally, enchanted to know you."

"Where do you learn such good Spanish?"

"You think it is good? I feel it is very poor."

"Your accent is poor, the words are fine." Sterling breathed deeply again. This was it, the game of the young. Something that would never be available to him at home again. There, he would return altered, different from the boy he was when he left. Here, with Claudia, who returned his play, he was that boy. Young Billy. He smiled at her.

"I will try a better accent."

"I am joking; your pronunciation is good."

"I learned in school. Also, there are many people who speak Spanish where I am from."

"Ah, yes! I learn my English in school as well."

"Try some on me."

"Good. Hello, how are you? I am fine. My name is Claudia and I am happy to meet you." She postured up, "And. . ."

"Your accent was poor," Sterling replied.

"Billy!"

"No, no. It was good. Listen, do you go to school here?"

"No, I live in Triunfo. It is a pueblito east of here. My University is in San Miguel, near there."

"How is it?"

"It is beautiful. You should visit."

"I will."

"I must return. There will be more tourists soon."

"Yes, but return."

"I will," she said.

Sterling watched her leave. He began drinking his coffee more quickly, anticipating refills.

Suddenly, Roge came up to him. "Señor Sterling, I have found you. You like the café?"

"More than you know, Roge. What happened?"

"Nothing, Señor. I remembered an expression. I wanted to tell you."

"Please."

"It goes, 'Chucho no come chucho, y si come no come mucho.' "

"And what does it mean?"

"It means, dogs do not eat dogs," said Roge, with a shrug.

"Thank you, Roge. I feel more fluent already."

Claudia returned after a while. There were others at adjacent tables, and she hopped from one to another, chancing to look over at Sterling between stops and pleasantries and delivering coffee.

"And so, señor Billy, how do you go?"

"Fine. Claudia, can I know about you?"

"I do not understand the sentence."

"Tell me about Triunfo."

"I want to, but I am busy. There are many here today, look."

"I can see. And so, perhaps we can take dinner."

Claudia's smile didn't rescind, but it twitched a bit into

realization. She looked down at Sterling, a studious look, as if he was a textbook in a complicated class. She was also no stranger to the attention of male tourists.

"Where did you come from before here?" she asked.

"Iraq."

"Is it a bad place?"

"No. It is just hot. Listen, what about the dinner?"

"I do not think so."

"I will tell of Iraq and you will tell of Triunfo."

"I'm sorry Billy. I do not think I can."

Billy sat back in his chair, again leaning back on the hind legs. He said then, in English, "Then I will wait here until the evening, and you'll serve me dinner, and it will be as if you said yes."

"More slowly, more slowly, please," Claudia said, with a smile.

"I said I will stay here until dinner, teaching you English word by word."

The water moved below him in its prescribed manner. The rise of a wave appeared so far out to sea that he knew it was coming, and when the lip separated from the rest, sucking in its stomach to curl and tumble over, Sterling was where he needed to be. He caught it and stood. The ocean propelled him along the shoreline while he ran his fingers along the translucent green wall at the back of the tunnel. Sterling could not help himself but smile. His knee didn't even hurt. And deep inside of him, beyond consciousness, dwelt a realization that he could come through this all right. That he could return home with no more than an aching knee to show for his time away. What seemed impossible a week before now suggested its potential: he could survive his life.

He couldn't help himself. Each morning, he'd arrive at the same café early, and talk with Claudia before taking his rented board to the ocean. He didn't stay that first evening, despite his playfulness. Rather, he determined to return each day. His goal was unclear. He knew it was common for men on leave to gravitate toward women, especially women from foreign countries, but what he felt for Claudia wasn't romance, nor was it lust. She intrigued him, because she was the opposite of where he'd come from, blemish free. He didn't want her, at least not any more than he'd ever wanted any beautiful woman; he wanted to sit and talk with her. If she told him to climb to the top of one of the distant mountains with her and live, he'd agree. There, he'd watch her mole elevate and fall as she spoke a tightrope of two languages, mingled in their common hybrid tongue. And yes, he admitted to himself, then he'd kiss her. He'd move the brown hair from her front to her back.

Claudia told him of Triunfo, of her Godfather, a former FMLN soldier who now took in stray dogs; his back yard was a zoo of dogs in various stages of regaining their health. She told him that El Salvador was called the *country of hammocks*, and that if there was an earthquake at night, half the country wouldn't know, swaying sleepily as they were. She told him that she was the *Reina de Triunfo* some years back, and that *Vaca Negra* was putting Coca Cola in a plastic sandwich bag with a dollop of ice cream and biting the corner open, to squirt it in one's mouth.

He told her of Southern California, how hard it was to grow grass there. How there were places along the coast where mountains blocked the view of the setting sun, suggesting that it never really went anywhere.

Their conversations lasted in the small spaces of coffee refills, and by the time Sterling made it to the ocean, his heart would be beating feverishly from the caffeine, and other things.

He rode the wave to shore, and looking up, saw her sitting beyond the reach of the water. She wore a long white dress that hung to her feet from the bent knees tucked into her chest. He approached her.

"You are watching me."

"You ride well."

"It is nothing," he said. He sat next to her, letting the surfboard drop away from them. "Tell me about your Godfather again."

"The dogs?"

"I am very interested in the dogs. But tell me about the FMLN."

Claudia didn't move but was noticeably reserved.

Sterling continued, "Listen, I am sorry. I don't know why I asked."

"It is because you are a soldier," Claudia said, "and in things such as war all soldiers have interest."

"I am not emotional about it."

"No," she said, turning to him. She smiled again; it was

genuine, despite the memories that wanted it to retire deep into her face, "but you would like to know."

"Yes."

"I do not remember much about the Civil War. I was very young when there was fighting. But I remember when I had eight years of age. . ."

"Listen, Claudia, you do not have to say anything. I am just as content to teach you English."

"Teach me English tomorrow, Billy. Now I will tell you about when I had eight years of age." She lay back on her elbows, each making a divot in the sand. Sterling watched her. "The father of my friend was an FMLN soldier. He was a good father to my friend and a good husband to the mother. I didn't know what the FMLN was, nor did I know that he was a soldier. It was not something that was talked about. He was there for my coronation. I was dressed in a pink gown and had a crown. I walked the length of Triunfo, among all of the people I had known all my life. My friend walked with me, and he walked behind, seemingly protecting us.

"Later that year, I was playing with my friend in their house. They had two buildings. From the front, her mother ran a small store of food and supplies. The building in the back was where they slept. Between, was a small court of grass, where we'd laugh; young girls, you understand."

"I understand," Sterling replied.

Claudia looked into the ocean; she grew quiet, but continued her story, "He played guitar from a hammock, singing quiet songs from the hills. He had a beautiful voice, and strummed the chords with his fingers so softly that we would have to lean in to hear.

"That day, my friend and I played upon the grass when. . . when things happened very quickly."

"Claudia. . ."

"It is okay señor Billy. This was long ago. Very quickly, men came in. They wore uniforms and guns. Not like the uniform you wear, but uniforms the color of trees. They marched in and surrounded the father of my friend. He lay still in the hammock, smiling at them, softly playing chords. My friend huddled close to me and I held her. We both had much fear. And the rest was quick. A man from behind, who held a machete, pulled the head of the father by the hair from the hammock and struck twice at the neck. What I remember is the wink of the father of my friend that stayed in the air while the rest of his body fell back into the hammock."

"*Guiño?*"

"It is to close one eye," Claudia said, miming it by touching closed her left eye with a finger.

"Oh. That is *wink* in English. You said he winked?"

"Yes. He winked at us, I thought."

"Terrible."

"It is terrible, and it is all that I know of the Civil War. It is what I remember of it. But that is not the worst."

"What is worst?"

"The fear."

"What fear?" Sterling asked.

"The fear I have today. Like looking at a head that winks. *Tengo miedo de muchas cosas, cosas benignas.*"

I have many fears, fears of benign things.

"Like what, for example?" Sterling asked, though he knew exactly what she meant. He had those fears as well. Traumas. Winking bodiless heads. Deep sharp knee pains.

"Airplanes, flying. Earthquakes (I feel them). Storms. Dogs; I cannot go into my Godfather's back yard. Buses. I have fear of these things. And others."

"Maybe they are things worth fearing," Sterling said.

"No. They are from when I had eight years of age. It stays with me. It shows me things to fear. It gives me fears. Do you understand, Billy?"

"I understand." Sterling leaned back on his elbows, as she had been on hers. The ocean continued to roll as it always had. The sand beneath them radiated heat from the sun above, and it warmed them comfortably. Sterling took a chance and covered her hand with his. She looked over at him. On her face was a strange expression. She looked afraid and confused. She had the face of an eight-year-old child wondering why she would always bear the weight of what the world offered.

With that same face, she said, "Tell me of your war."

"I know little of it, really."

"You are not so young."

"I am. Truly, Claudia, I am just as young as you. But we do not have machetes. We have guns. And we fire them into the dark."

"Without knowing what is in the dark?"

"Yes. Without knowing."

The rest of the week passed in a similar way. There were many cups of coffee, caught waves, and longer and longer moments of silence between them, when they would muse introspectively and separately about what their relationship meant.

She was a young student.

He a soldier.

And that simplicity made it apparent that whatever they were was terminal.

But Claudia did not fear him, and that kept her interest. As for Sterling, he awoke each day with a hunger to see her. It was the same as stomach hunger, which propels young men from their beds; but with Claudia, her presence was enough to stop the ache.

Then, Claudia went home to Triunfo for a few days. In her absence, Sterling's hunger grew. Gliding upon the waves had not the same calming affect for him that it did when Claudia had been there days before. Roge's expressions were less engaging. He would sit astraddle his board and look toward the shore, hoping to see her in a long white dress walking to the point where ocean met beach, water to land, where he could glide in to meet her.

"I will go AWOL," he thought to himself. "I will leave, and I will take her, like a riptide, to the top of the highest mountain. That's it, Pal, right to the top. We'll lie in the bed of a pick-up and climb until the air is thin and the sun is close, and we'll watch all the world go on below. They won't miss me enough to come find me." Sterling drummed on the board with his fingertips, excited at the prospect.

The absurdity of the thought comforted him. Why not? Why couldn't he simply leave it behind him? His leave. His leaving. What was the alternative? The rest of his tour? Screeching knee pains and the wailing whistles of shells? Running, where each step in the sand wrenched his leg and twisted the knee so that the failing cartilage underneath dissolved more and more? And then, if he was lucky, home? That other desert? A place that would become foreign to him when he returned? Put so plainly, the choice seemed obvious; the scales weighted heavily to a side.

Claudia came back. She arrived at La Libertad by bus in the early afternoon.

In their unintentional excitement, they hugged each other for the first time, withdrawing with young smiles and dropped awkward eyes.

"I am happy to see you," she said.

"Equally."

"I do not know why, Billy. It is strange. I told my mother of you."

"And what did she say?"

"She said what mothers say."

"Which?"

"That I am young. That I am so young."

"The mother is correct."

"Of course. But listen, Billy. I do not work today, and I have fear that you are to leave soon."

"Do not be preoccupied."

"Can we do something today?"

"Yes. What?"

"You say."

"I say let us go for a swim." Claudia's face relaxed and she looked down.

"El mar me llevará." *The ocean will take me.* It was the second time he'd heard the expression. It translated peculiarly. Directly, it could also mean, *the ocean will wear me*, like clothing. Sterling knew the meaning of the expression, but could not fight the concept laced into the double entendre. The ocean wearing her, wearing him, as they wore it when they surfaced, dripping with a part of it, discarding it in the cotton of warm towels.

"I will not let it," he said.

She relented, "Promise me, Billy."

"I promise you."

They approached the ocean. Claudia stepped tentatively as the dry sand became the matted wet foyer of the water. She looked at Billy and smiled insincerely, trepidatiously.

"I promise," he said, and dove into the water. He surfaced and looked back at her, as if to show her it was safe. He smoothed back hair that wasn't there. She stood looking at him blankly.

He knew the face. In it he saw the eight-year-old girl's fear, the trauma she wore the way the ocean would wear her if she swam out too far and the riptide took her. He stood, the water only up to his knees, the smallest waves thudding against the back of his legs.

Between them was the barrier of land and sea: her life damaging her; his, him.

Claudia turned and ran back toward the buildings clustered on the coast.

Sterling let the waves thud against the back of his knees. He watched her run, and knew there was no mountaintop. Cartilage does not regenerate. The ocean is the same no matter where one steps into it. Once things were done, they were done. He would go back to the desert.

por Rosa Elena, Leo, Claudia, y Noel: mi familia guanaco

Self-Portrait

She's in the paper again. It isn't as if she shouldn't be, but I can't help feeling something wrong, something deeply strained, about seeing her face again: black-and-white 3 X 5, at a community service project she was involved in some years back. It's written there as plain as the ink, yet another article chronicling such a young—such a short—life. I should feel—I *do* feel—remorse at it all, at the degradation of our society, but all I can think about are all the 3 X 5 black-and-whites that aren't in the paper today.

The others.

The apartment they gave me is just off the 46th Street station in Sunnyside, around the corner from a pawn shop and one of those Styrofoam-cup coffee deals that put the cup in a paper bag before you walk out the door. The Bureau wants its agents as near the scene as possible, so I get holed up where the every-few-minute squealing of the elevated brings me out of any revelry worth keeping and has me peer out the window: fire escape, bricks-with-powdering-seams, plummet, ground. I peel back the plastic perforated tab of the lid and drink the first sip of the coffee. I have a desk I keep neat and organized, a simple file folder full of charts, biographies, and testimony; and a lamp surrounded in green glass, so pretty you'd think it Tiffany's, that lights up Amber's face, her statistics, and the crime scene where her blood marks the sidewalk slab to remind us where all that's supposed to be inside of us comes out.

I'm also collecting every newspaper article written about the case. From the simple first report: a mugging, a girl shot; to the more recent profiling: her career, her friends, her good (best) deeds. I keep them all, a running journalistic reel of everyone's darling victim. And there I go, the man sent to solve the crime, so sarcastic that it sickens me. I see my daughter in Amber, just like everyone does. She's the archetypal every-girl for America, and her death makes us furious. Her face, near daily, populating the pages of our papers.

I'll catch them. That's why they sent in the FBI. This isn't just a case for one small rural family who lost their daughter on the streets of Queens, but for the whole of America, that needs closure from barbarousness, that needs to sink their teeth back into the animal kingdom and keep it afraid at the borders of civilization. The last article they'll ever write about Amber will have my quote in it; it won't satisfy the nation, because it won't make sense; but then again it *will* satisfy them, enough for them to wake up the next day and read something else in the papers.

I move around the apartment slowly. There's something in the revolutions and pacing that makes me think. I know I get just a few minutes before another train screams by, so I walk the room intently, instinctively, thinking my next move. Amber's murderer is not a criminal mastermind. Nine times out of ten they are junkies looking for quick means. It won't take long to put Federal heat on enough ne'er-do-wells in the neighborhood to get a few directions as to where I need to go. There's also the reward—funds raised piecemeal by the cops, the family, the media, philanthropists—the reward that inflates and rises with the hours, fat as an indulgent balloon, forever elastic in its spread. So I'm not thinking of my next move; I'm thinking about Amber, about what it is about her that means so much. So much that the NYPD ceded to the FBI for a mugging.

I came in from a Manhattan train just over a week ago. The NYPD gave me the file, a photocopied collection of clues that, when assembled, would make a puzzle box top so clear that it may as well have been a map with an enormous X leading to Amber's killer. On the thirty-minute train ride to Queens I read almost all of the evidence and realized my being there was a symbolic gesture. I should have known it, the way the police chief handed me the file with a smirk, as if they'd already figured out the case and my suit, my credentials, my being, were superfluous. I was there only because the people needed to know that the Federal Government was interested in Amber's case. A twenty-three year old white girl from upstate, a college grad, an impending architect, studied in Europe a year almost directly after war's end. The whole continent was still a bunch of ruts and people trying to piece together the apocalypse that was the violence, and even so, there Amber was, country-hopping from restored France even into smoldering Germany. I suppose the architecture of Europe was, for her, a valued commodity for study.

She was stereotypically pretty; the articles had to make a constant mention of it. Blond. Blue eyes. Wide smile glinting off the distinct newspaper feel of the page. She had friends, she had beaus. She had bought a new purse in Manhattan the evening of her death, and as she left the station I'd rumble into a few minutes later, a man grabbed that new purse and fired one round, point blank, at her chest. She died at the bottom of the elevated station's stairs.

I got off that stop and walked down those stairs after closing her file on the train. The crime scene had been well-documented already: photos taken, shell marked then filed; of course the stairwell had been again open to the public. It was peculiar to see so many people walking by, up and down the steps, unaware of what had happened there just over a week before. Strange that I stood there too, life moving on as if it never happened. The sidewalk slab didn't even have a stain anymore.

But, of course, it did happen. Whether they realized it or not, everyone knew about Amber. Everyone talked about her, not just in Queens, but everywhere. She made national news. This pretty young architect, who traveled the war-torn world to gain an inspiration for her craft, who had so much hope and such a bright future, was gunned down mercilessly for a cheap purse she didn't even have long enough to put anything valuable inside. And now the FBI was there to erect the appropriate gallows.

The night I arrived someone else was killed in Queens. I don't know, maybe a number of people were killed that night. This middle-of-the-century gun play seemingly extending outward in every direction from urban centers into the aching tendrils of squalor at the extremities of every city. But the reason I remember this one person being killed is because it happened so near where Amber had been. Another apparent mugging, only a block or two away. And this neighborhood is called Sunnyside. Being that I am here to solve a murder, I went to the crime scene as soon as I heard about it. I thought there may be evidence to link the two crimes, or perhaps I just thought it my job to investigate. A murder is a murder, after all. I am of a profession that must investigate these things regardless of where it happens or who it happens to.

I genuinely used to believe that.

When I arrived at the scene there were two police officers. They stood erect, talking, the body already long gone. They laughed together. There were no photographers in sight. I stopped to speak with them.

"Another murder," I said.

"Yeah," one officer said, "You here working on the Amber What's-her-name case, yeah?"

"Donnelly."

"Come again, friend."

"Donnelly. Amber's last name."

"Right, yeah. Donnelly. That's it. Hard to forget when it's in the papers every day."

"That's so," I replied. Then, "So what do we have here?"

"Well I doubt you're going to find evidence here that links to Amber. To Donnelly. This is just one of those everydayers."

"What do you mean?"

"Come on, friend. Don't tell me they don't educate you FBI fellows about how things work out here. How long you been around anyway?"

"Long enough." It was my first case. "So tell me what you mean."

They took a long look at one another, and the officer who had been speaking to me spoke again, "I mean this is one of those things that happen. Every day. Kid, probably selling drugs, gets shot probably by someone whose turf he's on." The other cop studied me as if for reaction.

There was more to the conversation, but it's not necessary to recant it here. All I should add is that, when I turned to leave, the first officer called after me, "Don't worry, you won't read about him in tomorrow's paper."

And he was right.

My small room in Sunnyside also has a phone. Through it, tips filter in after having been screened for red herrings by the NYPD. Today I've received two good ones. It's that reward money, really; some friend-of-a-friend knows someone who knows someone who saw so-and-so at somebody-else's place talking about "staying low for a while: Feds on to this one." I call a tipster back and he even says, "Shot the wrong chick, yeah? Most junkies 'round here know not to aim white."

I thank him for his information, ensure the reward with a successful prosecution, lay down the receiver, and scratch notes into my book; aware that I'll be able to pack up and head back to Manhattan within a day or two.

I pick the phone back up and dial the number for the downtown police chief who handed over Amber's file.

"Chinski."

"Hello, Chief. It's Special Agent Harper, out in Queens. Amber Donnelly case."

"Agent Harper, yes. Getting close?"

"Very."

"That's good. Reward's getting so high I bet the killer's family is waiting like at an auction for the high bid to rat their own fellow out."

"Listen, I've got a question for you."

"Alright."

"Yesterday, when I arrived, there was another shooting, just around the corner from Amber's."

"Probably unrelated, Harper."

"Yes. I mean, I know. I was calling concerning this murder."

"And."

"Well, I wanted—I was wondering if there were any leads on that case."

"Leads?"

"Yes. Have the investigators found anything out about who shot that young man?"

"Investigators?"

"Chief Chinski?"

"Listen, Agent Harper, how long you been around?"

"Long enough." Rosy cheeks. Wet behind ears. Short in the tooth. Whatever.

"I see," he chuckles. "Listen, you have any idea how many black men are shot in Queens in a year? In the whole city? In the country? You think we have the manpower to investigate every single one? You think we have enough reward money for all of them? Word to the wise, Harper, stick to Amber. There ain't any investigators."

"But—."

"And Harper, another thing."

"Yes?"

"We're handling it. We handle all of them. Every day with them. Stick to Amber."

We hang up.

The green-glassed lamp brings out the pretty contours of Amber's face. They only ever print photos of her smiling; they only ever shoot her white face against the contrast of a black background, maybe to emphasize her most prominent of features: that skin.

I have doors to knock on, but my conversation with Chinski leaves me unsettled, so I call my supervisor in Manhattan.

"What?"

"He was shot just a block or so from where Amber was."

"So?"

"Sir, I wanted to know if I could pick up that case as well. The Donnelly case is all but wrapped up."

"Then wrap it up, Harper. I'm sure the local cops can handle it."

"But Sir—"

"Harper?"

"Yes, sir."

"That's enough."

And we too, hang up.

I used to think the immune system was outside of the body, like a shield: protecting us from all the viruses and cancers and weapons of the outside world. When I say I used to think this I mean when I was a kid. I used to imagine an immune system, my immune system, glowing in an amorphous yellow around my body like a fluid suit, thick and impenetrable. I almost took pride in it, the fact that my body had such a genius method of protection that circled it and contained it and allowed in only the things that were necessary, like breath and sunlight. Even long after I outgrew these childish notions, came to understand how inside our immune systems are—all cells and marrow—I still liked to think of it as exterior. It was a shield, a badge. And I used this as motivation all throughout and up until I became an agent. I wanted to be the badge, the shield, the protector of society; to render it immune to all things that weren't breath and sunlight. I wanted—idealistic, sure, but there are worse things—to be the amorphous yellow that caught the things, fastball to mitt, that wanted our entire way of life to fall down.

But it becomes clearer and clearer to me what it means that our immune systems are inside, that they fight disease only when it infiltrates the body. It waits, idle, for the virus, and then only hopes— often in vain—it can purge. And so I can't help but wonder, is this me? Am I idle? Am I to rid the impurities of this body of people stuck living together only when we become sick enough to know something must be done, must be fought? Am I less a shield and more a system of flowing cells, born in bone, circling a body (perhaps yes, like on subway tracks) until I happen to encounter something rotten? Or is it worse? Does the body discriminate what ailments I should try to rectify? Is my amorphous yellow truly an amorphous red, one that seeks out only the disease the body deems to be the most important to combat? Because really, it's no great thing to be selective; because while the body has me fighting its select disease only, it's still dying from the ignorance of the others. But maybe the immune system doesn't get to choose; maybe the body *does* think it knows which diseases to fight. Which murderers to pursue. And maybe that's why despite our immune systems, we still die.

I walk around Calvary Cemetery because it's close and there's nothing to do. Earlier today, I found Amber's killer. There will be another round of newspaper articles, a press conference or two— that's why eloquence classes were so important at the Academy—a few testimonies from Amber's family, and then, the ether. Beyond an update, months hence, about the fate of her killer, there will be little more. Our world will move on. It was as I had suspected: a man desperate for drugs, so much so that I almost felt sorry for him and for cuffing him while a cousin, or such, flashed a smile of dollar signs then, thinking I might be stingy with the reward (mistaking that I, the arresting agent, would be administering said reward) made sure he would, indeed, be getting it. I gave him the number to call. We didn't much speak, Amber's murderer and I. I loaded him into a police car and like that, he was gone.

Walking around the cemetery seems natural to me. I know Amber isn't buried here and honestly, I'm not really thinking of Amber or that poor desperate fellow with the shadow of a noose following him. I'm here because the cemetery marks a distinct separation from city street, and really, we're all going to end up in here, or the like, eventually, so I might as well get used to it. I know that's morose and I don't mean to be. Just hours ago, I caught the man the entire country was looking for; I should feel at least that victorious. Amorphous yellow. But really, really—what I can't stop thinking about are all those faces that won't be, won't *ever* be, in the newspaper. No matter how they're killed, they won't be worth the ink.

The ordered rows of headstones seem almost clean in their design. I imagine, from above, you could line the rows nicely on the sharp edge of a ruler. It is green and it is stone but it is not the stone of the city: paved and flattened into sidewalk and road; rather, the stone is three-dimensional, huge outcroppings of marble and granite shapes, tilted perpendicular, as if all the sidewalk slabs stood up, bore their stains, and in showing the earth and grass, told the city: *no matter how much you build, you are still this underneath*. And the city responds:

we are at the middle of the century, it is 1952, at the triangular point of a see-saw; balanced toward the future is everything we can build and everything we will build. And, as if to prove it, the Brooklyn-Queens Connecting Roadway bisects the cemetery in an awful platform where cars cut the dead rest in two.

I rest after walking for what seems like the entire day. A monolith, a monument of sorts, erects itself toweringly from amidst other stones and is flanked on all sides by patina-green soldiers, frozen in their sculpted, rudimentary stances of looking out—surveying—an open field or impending regiment or rushing death. I rest there, back against the stone, and gaze out over the Manhattan skyline.

"Do you muse, too?" a voice asks from behind. Startled, I turn to see a man likewise sitting against the monument. He must have been on the other side when I arrived, but had revolved around enough that we are adjacent.

"Pardon me?"

"The city. You seem rapt in its attention." He nods toward the skyline. I follow from his face to the buildings.

"Oh. That. Well, yes. I suppose. But I am not musing. That is to say, I'm not thinking."

"I've never known a man to not think."

"Come again?"

"Perhaps the Buddhist monks can, resounding their mantras in loops. Not think, that is. But I've never known a man who can do it."

I bring my gaze back to his face, "Do I..."

"Know me? No. Nor I you. I just find it more awkward, I suppose, for two men to sit against the same edifice in silence in a graveyard in Queens than to say hello."

"I see, Mr....?"

"Clark. Jackson Clark."

We shake hands, "I'm Roman Harper."

"It's good to meet you."

"Likewise."

Despite his insistence of the potential awkwardness of men rapt with the attention of a city silhouette in a silent graveyard, we become, again, silent. The kinetic energy of the city all around has a fierceness to it that does, through perforations (entrances and exits to overpasses) find us, though the serenity is truly only threatened by what is inside of me. That same discomfort I haven't been able to shake since riding the train in from Manhattan.

"You know, it's funny," I say, commandeering his attention once again, "I've lived and worked in this city my entire life, and this is my first time in Queens. I just realized that."

"Imaginary borders anyway."

"You mean?"

"Just that what is Queens or Brooklyn or the whole United States is really just some unfortunate history, delusions of grandeur, and a cartographer's prejudice." His poetic eloquence stalls my response; it gives him just enough time to continue, "So then what brings you to Queens this first time, Mr. Harper?"

"A case."

"A case?"

"Maybe you've heard of it. Amber Donnelly?"

He nods with certainty, rubs his chin, "How could I not, indeed? It was close to here. I, myself, live close to here. You are, then, a detective?"

"FBI."

"FBI? I didn't realize this had become a Federal manner."

"It does when the nation mourns."

"Yes, yes. When the nation mourns," he says.

"May I ask you, Mr., I'm sorry."

"Clark. Jackson Clark."

"Mr. Clark. What do *you* do for a living?"

"I'm retired."

"Retired? Pardon me if I seem intrusive, but you seem a rather young man for retirement." Although perhaps twenty years my senior, Mr. Clark could easily have worked another twenty.

"Well, let's say I'm retired from the work I want to do, the work I was meant to do."

"May I ask?"

He reaches his hand out and rests it upon the leg of one of the gazing bronze soldiers. "I was an Assistant Professor of Chemistry at Harvard."

"Harvard! I hear that's an up-and-coming institution."

He laughs, "And right you are, Mr. Harper."

"As I said, Mr. Clark, I'm not a detective, but I do have an inquisitiveness. I hope you don't mind."

"It is better than the silence, yes?"

"Well, if you don't mind me asking..."

"Why am I retired from the work I was meant to do?"

"If you're willing."

"I suppose so, Mr. Harper. I suppose I am willing. I am retired because I quit teaching. I quit after the war, a couple of years back. A student of mine, you'd have heard of him…brilliant mind, knew the most keen things as if he'd seen them before we'd teach him; well, he did a terrible thing, and I bear some of that blame." I wait to indicate he can feel free to continue, and he does, "It was this terrible thing that my teaching allowed him to do, in the way that teachers, no matter how distant or far removed, are always responsible for their pupils, for what they do when they are beyond him."

"I'm not sure I follow."

"He was in my chemistry class, Mr. Harper. This bright young fellow. And I did what was contractually obligated of me. I taught him chemistry. And he left from my class and did a terrible thing with the chemistry I taught him. Applied it in all the wrong ways; so, by extension it is I who have done this thing."

"What did he do that was so terrible?"

"What did he do? I think you already know, Mr. Harper."

"What do you mean?"

"You were sent to Queens to look for Amber Donnelly's killer, yes?"

"Yes."

"Well, it was he who killed her."

I begin to think that this Mr. Clark may, for all his eloquence, not be entirely here, and in the way one reacts to lunacy by placating all the violence out of it, I begin to think of my departure while allowing him enough space to finish his tale and be quit without it seeming disrespectful.

"I hardly think the man I handcuffed this morning went to Harvard, Mr. Clark."

His face flickers in the realization that Amber's killer has been caught; even this man has invested himself in the poor young girl who left us as do our most pleasant dreams.

"Indeed that man most certainly didn't, Mr. Harper. But although *that* man pulled the trigger that killed Amber, it was Julius, my Julius, who really killed her, who killed us all. Killed us with fear and finality and the ability to end all that is and ever was or will be human. Julius may have not been directly responsible for her death, but it is his terrible thing that makes her life, her history, and her legacy so delicate that the next small irresponsibility will erase it from the Earth. And not just Amber's but everybody's."

"I'm not sure I follow you, Mr. Clark."

"Indeed. I'm speaking in vagaries. My apologies, Mr. Harper. It is the shame of what Julius has done that forced my retirement, my vow to never teach chemistry to another soul again. It is the shame that brings me here, to this monument, daily, to look out over the skyline that is so beloved, and may someday soon not exist. Julius worked at the bequest of the government, and he succeeded to give them what they wanted: a beast charged in metal casing, never again dormant, to erase precisely what it no longer wanted to see. That's what the government wanted, what it asked Julius to complete: to erase the populations of the planet it didn't like. And Julius, using what we taught him, built."

Newspapers always feel a little still-wet. It's not that their paper dryness isn't obvious; it's the way they leave a little bit of themselves on your fingers that reminds you of how water—fresh from faucet or dipped in ocean—stays a little on skin.

In the Manhattan office, a week after receiving the hyperbolic congratulations of colleagues celebratory in the false-gratuitousness of accomplishing some great thing that is truly such a small thing, I read the daily paper. There is no mention of Amber. How quickly the national attention loses focus from its obsessions; how interested it is in the wrapped-up tight bow of conclusion, only to pass on to something else to qualify as zeitgeist. The tattoo that was Amber Donnelly has become a lessening bruise evolved from ugly purple to amorphous yellow, just under the skin, fading too quickly to believe, into nothing. I'm already on another case, my second.

The newspaper spills its crimes; its contents a roll call of atrocities, but all I can see is the grey between the black lines. I can't read the black words or look at the black pictures because I'm so distracted by the negative space between the print. If you look at any printed document, even the one I'm writing right now, the words seem to take on a lifted dimension from the space of the page; but you can reverse their demand, have them fade into the background, and read, instead, the empty space of grey from which they spring. It is in these empty spaces that the stories of the streets whisper. It is in these spaces, the greys beyond the ink, where people are murdered by bullets, then murdered by silence. It is here, our nation turns a collective head away.

And a byline from today's edition, tucked into a corner, that I catch almost by accident, reads, "Nagasaki: Effects of Radiation Still to be Determined." And below, a few lines along, the article continues, "Architects of the weapon cannot be located for comment."

Mr. Friend

The home was called The Villages, though it was a singular structure and on the seam of the city and its nearest suburb, and was in a neighborhood called Chestnut Hill, though there was no hill and the chestnut trees had either been lumbered long ago or had been nothing but a romance in the first place. A green-railed bridge wed the ridges of the Wissahickon ravine by the trail head to the park. Trailhead, he thought, or trail end, depending on the orientation of the walker. He drove over.

The trees on either side betrayed the fact that the road upon which he drove was paved only after felling a number of their fellows; the entire city, he thought, was once this woodland, where all that remains of its native people was a stone statue deep off the trail—white and commissioned by a wealthy, nearby neighbor—that covered, with saluting hand, the brow of his forehead against the sun or against the divinity that brought to his woods saviors with saws. He looked up and out of the windshield; the bare winter branches set against the sky like the bronchial tubes of anatomy textbooks: trees and lungs on opposite sides of breath.

They'd cut down the trees because no one had reverence for trees even though they gave life, as all things progeny underestimate the vitality breathed from paternity. Never more climbed, sheltered under, never more rested against nor slept amongst, never again scratching the backs of bears nor sharpening the tusks of elephants, never more shadowing the sun nor describing the wind, never living nobly: satisfied of their roots and place—this shaved Earth a razor burn of stumps, and yet it is the *people* who now tramp the open ground like amputees.

The hopeless, antiseptic smell reminded him of the sacristy. A sign reading *The Villages* was illuminated from behind by buried lights behind the letters, the one behind the second *L* out, emphasizing the last two syllables by its shade. There was a man in a wheelchair by the fireplace in the lobby where flames ate the empty space above themselves, and his eyes refocused from the eating to the man who'd just walked in and was signing the register. When the eyes of the chair-bound man met the eyes of the visitor, there was at the same moment a plea and a fear: the yearning came from the wish (not the only wish but the deepest) that he'd be the visited, and the fear came from the vestments. The black. The sterility and stoicism. Priests only showed their faces around there when someone was close to death, though the joke on them—on all—was the proximity at which death always waited.

But it was true: the priest was there for Last Rites. It was a trail end.

"Hello," the priest said. This would be his last sacrament. He was old enough, too old, for it anymore, and so would retire after performing the Anointing of the Sick on the man in the bed before him; it was his last sacrament, the end of a long life of administering such sacraments, and he would withdraw to a quiet home—not unlike this one—and wait for his own priest to come. The room told of faux home: carpeted in colors not easily stained and wood paneling at the edges that looked less like wood when approached and hotel-style lamps and prints in frames and the lavatory with stainless steel rails around the toilet and bath and the one beeping machine the thing out of place. There was no hum to the room, no life, no vibration. It was a holding pattern, a cell, into which were placed people for whom medical advancement stalled the natural progress of the body, for a time. So much had been spent on the extension of life, only to find little for it to extend into. These rooms, all rooms like it, multiplied across the country, to hold medicine's greatest accomplishment—life everlasting, ticking hearts in limp bodies, and to be a priest in all of that science felt just a little validating, as if the net gain of corporeality still came laughably short of the old thing, of faith.

He said hello to the man lying in bed before him but the man did not answer. The priest pulled the single chair of the room to the edge of the bed and sat. "Hello," he said again. "Do you know me? Do you remember me?"

"Mr. Friend," the man said, looking at him with a clarity that the priest knew wasn't there. It hadn't been there for a time. The man was in the later stages, the last stages, of the disease that took his memory—the most unjust disease—where the body can live on while the mind whips in panic at an entire life seen through ever descending screens of increasing opaqueness.

"No," the priest said. "It's me."

But it was no use. The man puckered his lips against the toothless ridges inside and shook his head slowly, turning away. "Mr. Friend," the old man said again.

The priest sighed. He began.

In the name of the Father, and of the son,

The old man turned back at this start, at these words, as if startled, and mouthed again—this time with no sound—what seemed to be his only phrase.

and the Holy Spirit. Amen.

The priest took the man's hand, the skin phyllo thin and transparent, and held it gently. He rubbed his thumb against the knuckles, displaced the hair between them, sighed the resignation that comes when what was expected still strikes suddenly. He knew he had to continue the ritual but felt less adept than usual, as if the power of God, through which he worked, was somehow truncated at the bedside of this father, this power.

The peace of the Lord be with you always. The Lord is our shepherd and leads us to streams of living water. Coming together as God's family, with confidence, let us ask the Lord's forgiveness, for he is full of gentleness and compassion.

He was not a parent, but the moniker *father* taught him of that vantage. He leaned into the old man and kissed his cheek, "Do you know me?" The cheek was soft, the kiss wet lingering.

The faint almost breath, among the last of a long sequence, "Mr. Friend."

He knew then that a child would never love their parents the way or to the extent to which their parents loved them. But those parents did not love *their* parents the way or to the extent to which they were loved by them. Children would love their own children this way without this way or this extent being requited. It was this generational one-way comprehensive love that united parents and progeny; it was the love for one's child that completed the love felt for them by their own parents, which they never before truly understood.

"No," the priest said. He looked out of the window. There were no trees. "It's me, Dad. It's your son."

"Mr. Friend."

Praise to you, God the only-begotten Son. You humbled yourself to share in our humanity and you heal our infirmities. Through this holy anointing may the Lord in his love and mercy help you with the grace of the Holy Spirit.

Before the old, bed-ridden man was old, he bore a son, and loved him. On Sundays, his wife, a Christian, went to church; he went into the woods. There was a spirituality there, as if the Gnostic

Gospels's insistence of God in all things called him away from edifice and into the trees, where he could saunter for the hour when she was in a different prayer, she always bringing the child, always a church wall away from her husband but loving him no less. He brought his son often to the woods but it was the wooden rafters of the stonewalled church with dusted stained glass and martyred statues captured in their various agonies and the repetitive chants, songs cycling through celebrations, and stoicism of the priest before his congregation, that won the child. From a young age, his son wanted to follow into the cloth.

The man was raised in the church and married his wife in the church but when he became a father he stopped being a Christian because the Christian God could not be thus. The need for supplication. The conditional love. God: the essential third person omniscient absentee father. To father was no such thing. It was a verb. To father was to submit control to the will of the universe, not need omnipotence against it. To do it gladly. To understand that the act of creation made the creator *less* relevant, *less* sentient, *less* powerful. To accept the novelty of that reduced agency.

When his son took the Holy Orders, he gave his son an inscribed bible of sturdy leather and gold-embossed lettering—the epigraph, his heart.

Kilbourne Hole was where they did it, where the Earth sunk into itself, the basalt cliffs block-fragmented and arranged by the awesome power of angry things below the surface, a mile-wide ditch in desert offering no panacea from sun or thirst or refuge from travel but where the travelers rested anyway, the cliff edges' sinking feeling like enough an aberration of land to sink with it, be born to be killed, and breathe what was supposed to be freedom but felt no different than home, where they did it: took the child from his mother's nipple. The country's Attorney General went to church every Sunday, supplicated himself in front of the Lord and had the Ten Commandments framed and hung in his office in DC, exactly two-thousand miles from Kilbourne Hole where he'd never have to meet the woman or her son; he slept under a crucifix and prayed on knees in pajamas by a bed near the Capitol for goodness to enter his heart—he said it was about "deterrence."

The man's son had been a priest for a year, had delivered weekly homily in quaking voice, but quickly commanded himself in a faith that diluted doubt to nothing. He had traveled to New Mexico to make his body a vessel for the transport of water and prayer but was a fence between coyotes and snipers—the former gold-toothed and rank, the latter begging him to move out of the quadrants of their cross hairs. (They, too, Christians). His father was proud of his going there, of his human kindness—the one thing he wished of his son the day he was born: kindness in the face and wake of humanity. His father did not go to church, did not believe, but hugged his son at the airport, grabbed his neck behind the clerical collar and looked into his eyes saying, "I am proud of who you are," to which the son replied, "I hope only to bring some peace to those poor people," and the father nodded, pulled the son close, touched foreheads, and waved through the sliding doors where went his boy, grown, a father of sorts himself, to the West where he could hold people without country against the vilification privileged to patriotism.

He was in Kilbourne Hole when it happened.

And when he returned, more human, because he was more hurt by the world, he embraced his father and moaned into him, "They took the boy, right there, and put him in a van. Drove away."

The father squinted against the dark of his son's soutane.

"Her breast dribbled, as if it was looking for the mouth that had been wrenched from it."

He was weeping openly at the same airport where they had departed a month before.

"And I could do nothing. I pleaded, ran after the van, came to the woman and spoke to her, prayed for her, and it was nothing. Then another van came and took her, in handcuffs, without her son, a different way."

The two negotiated the transient personality of the airport, the space where nothing lived but life flashed match-head temporary.

"They call themselves Christians, Dad. Christians. They say they follow Christ then do this. This to people who don't even speak their language, can't understand what they're saying, why they're doing it. This basic human truth. To never take a child from a parent. But they say they are Christian. What am I doing? Me, a leader to them. A parent to them."

His father thought about what he said, the basic human truth. Wondered what he would have done had someone stolen his son from him. Wondered how he would survive.

"This hurts worse than anything I've felt." Christians hanging the cross itself on a cross of their own hatred in the name of a god-man who, if there, would have held the mother and child together against the most violent force.

It was Kilbourne Hole that first tested his son's faith, and it would take a father's selflessness to restore it. A conversion.

He told his son, "The worst kind of fear is an abstract fear." It was something a father should never have to explain to a son: that there was ugliness in the world and it would surround him and try to get in and it would likely get in but what he wanted most was to help his son develop a skin against it. Like the skin he gave of himself. But it permeated and we must watch the crude innocence be eaten by it, a cancer that catalyzed the final transformation to full person: to lose faith in people. He said, "Our country's coasts, I'm sorry, are parentheses that sometimes hold an aside of hate." Fathers were men, too.

Soon after, in an awkward moment in the very woods to which his father retreated and where he raised him, when they had reached the part of the trail that felt closed-in enough by trees (it was faux, but if they breathed deeply at that exact spot, they could just believe that the air those trees provided made the inhale somehow fresher) there, the son asked his father to call him *father*. He didn't ask for the validation commiserate with naming; it was a deeper petition. The Wissahickon woods were sacred in that they smelled of their owness: wet brittle rock and leaves cycling through the dying and fertilizing of new growth, the trails soggy with the held dregs of past weather and scented similarly: of rain that was in a mud that stuck and a creek somewhere—the namesake—which called to the first from the ships to cut there, build there, make a city of that scent. Those first colonists knew the sacredness of those woods and knew the city that would occupy that space would somehow hold the same potency in rising from such a place. So the trees of that place became the lumber for the beams of the houses that would rise there, transmitting from tree to beam a sanctity inexorably attached to what quiet, woodly people could recognize as holy. In the moment he asked his father to call him *father* then asked him to join his flock, there was no force in his shepherd staff's ground strike, no urgency in his asking, because he knew paternity could not flow upriver. His father might call him the new name but it was only language, sound and code, and he could not hope to think of his father as his child or lamb. Nor could he believe his God capable of sending his father to damnation, sinner and nonbeliever though he might have been; it was, as if, in this man, God would make an exception for sacrilege.

Still, he wanted him saved.

His father knew that this was Kilbourne Hole sinking his son deeper, and that he had to do what was called of him, his own sacrament (brother to sacrifice), to father, a verb, his son.

He converted.

The deeper into the systems of man the further away from peace, the man knew. He came to his son's church every Sunday—no different than if he'd come to the ballpark where his son pitched—was baptized and confessed, knelt at the appropriate times and blinked when the holy water fled the aspergillum and coughed at the sage ghosts leaving the censor; he memorized the creeds and hummed through the homily, took the Eucharist, offered offerings, clasped his wife's hand, and pretended.

His son knew the conversion and attendance was for him, not for faith, but he was a priest who felt an insatiable responsibility for the members of his congregation, and so hoped for osmosis, that the spirituality of the building would seep into his father and bring him in. What he felt most deeply was the need to be with his father, that there could be no peace in heaven without him; he feared an eternity without his father where he, having failed to save the man he most needed to, would wander through paradise in the dread of this most precious lost soul burning. He was a good priest, respected and loved, and believed truly in his devotion to the church; he felt joy in seeing his father in the pew but realized it was only for support—bleacher cheering—and not a true belief. He thought of what he'd do as father to *his* congregation, if his children were wrenched from him. He wondered how far off love was from salvation, if any distance at all. Religion and biology, parenthood, the father preached and his father listened—what greater hope could mankind wish for to be a shield against the rot of itself?

* * *

Father in heaven, through this holy anointing grant my father comfort in his suffering. When he is afraid, give him courage, when afflicted, give him patience, when dejected, afford him hope, and when alone, assure him of the support of your holy people. We ask this through Christ our Lord.

All forgot that the miraculous city that rose and spread before them, with its bisections of time in the various architectures of colonial homes to corporate towers, was culled from a forest in a valley, with two rivers and a creek and their eternal flowing ignorant to the chopping of their bank trees and damming of their own bodies. In that city, the homes were built with shared walls between, brick being better than trees at shielding one's life from their neighbors.

Roots and schist, shadowed by dusk light, turned his ankle toward sprain and yet he proceeded directly to the place, the sky through winter branch striations a royal blue shade deepening to universe. The Wissahickon, last bastion of woodland against the imposition of city, showed little sign of the population density surrounding; no cars could be heard, no voices, none of the weep and lamentation of the priest as he walked to the place, having come from The Villages, having come from his last sacrament, having sat thumbing a thin-skinned hand as someone unplugged the out-of-place machine. It would be dark soon. The branches, finger skeletal. He was going to the place. On the inside of his coat he portaged the small book, gold-embossed, heavy in the odd off-balance weight on one side of the body: the text bearing everything to which he'd dedicated his life and something more than life, something metaphysical and unknowable and endless—it was faith in script and it was not to be challenged but it banged against his ribs, stopped no bullets, took from him no violence of loss, but reminded him of itself in its banging. His father had given it to him on the day he received his Holy Orders, became a father himself, and he took it and kept it and read from it all those years. Now, the darkening woods and precarious roots and schist threatened—they were not the pleasant reprieve of day, but something worse, sinister. No, he knew, trail-bound, momentous, agile for his age, done—it is only me that is this darkness. What I am of and by this virtue was of me is gone; these primordial woods care nothing. Yet he went on to the place.

"Dad, do you remember? Can you tell me who I am?" The home's staff hovered around the room, unsure of themselves in the face of a priest that was a child. All fathers were at first sons. The old man was in and out of consciousness, the machine removed from the room, all bodies still save for the hearts.

"Mr. Friend," he said, again. The priest breathed, defeated. The surface of the world was mottled with disease, desperate with despotism, a visage that would slow a growing man's faith for goodness. It was a sun that could never be known because it could not be seen but was ubiquitous in its warmth. Too long looking away from such a sun while still feeling it could turn a man from life, frustrate him against his fellows. It was a decaying and corrupting surface. But there was purity below. It must be held out for, dove for.

"Okay."

God our Father, we have anointed your child with the oil of healing and peace. Caress him, shelter him, and keep him in your tender care.

He was in the place.

It was a special place in the way that it was completely inconsequential to anyone but him and his father, the way the most banal place took special precedent over other geographies in the minds of those who found love there, who harvested indescribable energy from the feel of it and returned to feel the same energy because it was there that there was connection. Such places held the purity below, they must have, because how else could they bring so much peace in the otherwise tumult? (Passing a sidewalk bench in ignorance, it is heaven for someone.) His father, at the last, did not remember him. But in the place, the place in the woods where they would go, that didn't matter; they were both there, perpetually, in paradise. Home is, after all, just a place people agree to meet their family.

It had been years since he'd opened the book; he didn't need to; after so long, so much knowledge of it, the book was more a representation than words. But then he remembered his Holy Orders, his father's giving of the book, the epigraph within. He opened the cover and with a penlight read:

My son, on this day of your devotion, I hope you feel some of what a father feels for his child, that you know just some of the love.

When you were small, just born, for no reason whatsoever and with no rationality, I would call you Mr. Friend. *It was a pet name that fell from my mouth one day and stuck for some months but didn't mean anything. Now, in the strange way of things, I know how the accident of my calling you that came to fit you. You are a friend to the world.*

I am proud of you.
With Love,
Dad.

The Wissahickon woods held the last trees, which were the first trees. The place was sacred. The priest wept. The sick were anointed. The sacraments administered. Nothing was ever gone; the woods cared. It was full dark then but he felt no fear.

May God the Father bless you.
May God the Son heal you.
Amen.

Only Connect...

Connect without bitterness until all men are brothers.
—E. M. Forster

When the tusk of the flame rounded the back of the largest log, it seemed to curl beyond the surface of the wood rather than catch it. There was a snap, a partial collapse, an exhale of hot, black breath into the flue before the log's surface began to scorch, telling Edward that the flame had found purchase, that it had caught the largest log, was ready to reduce it into coal, to advance the notion that man could care for himself and provide warmth and light and could facilitate the random and incomprehensible chemical combustion essential to him in that it was essential to everyone. He reached for the nearby iron poker and, wielding it sword-like, duel-like, aimed a lunge toward the log's parry, but Morgan said, "Don't."

When she'd reached in earlier, Edward put down the spent charcoal that lay like residue from someone else's warmth and brushed her hand, as if to insist he could handle the making of the fire and as if to protect her hand from the phantom flame, long dead, from another evening. He left a soot smudge. Morgan wiped the black into her jeans, fading it greyer with each swipe, but it remained tattoo-like when she'd finished.

Their chairs faced the fireplace and each had a hardcover book on the respective arms. Edward had intended to "read more" on this trip and, having forgotten to bring any books of his own to satisfy this intention, found a book from one of the ubiquitous stacks of books randomly placed throughout the barn to give the impression that the city family's upstate getaway was a hamlet of quiet, intellectual study. Edward was grateful for the coy library as much as he was annoyed by the invisible family's pretension as much as he was envious of their barn their fireplace their books. He'd selected a book he thought was by an author he most *should* read and set to build the ambiance necessary to complete his fantasy: the upstate wilderness fireside literary observance; breathing burning wood and knowing peace. Morgan brought a book lent to her by a friend who'd recently delivered and so didn't need it anymore. Both lay unopened on the chairs' arms while Edward and Morgan watched and hoped for the fire's vitality.

Whatever the listing said, it was a barn. The two rooms, separated by a plank wall, were in the hayloft. The fireplace in the addition was made disingenuous by the differing stone that jutted gutlessly from the side of what must have been a far wall and, when they'd entered, despite the sprayed foam insulation between the boards and rafters, the winter draft kept with them. The strange transient need: to leave the city. The American Mecca where no one was born and no one died of old age, save for the few who'd only ever known the island—the planet's magnet; a gravity not toward the core but toward the clustering and rising of people on top of one another. To live there but to leave there. To need to. To find a remoteness within grasp. To cross bridges to the mainland and drive a few hours into the country in order to find what was once a barn (seams foam-filled) but can now be rented cheaply for sharing couples too timid to succumb to the struggle of the fire despite their hands never before setting it to wood. This dichotomy of Americana: the town and the country, the city and space, the wilderness and the wild; the dense dense dancing of the one, the open loneliness of the other.

The others set to gather wood, the boy to chase the dog, and Edward and Morgan had taken to starting the fire. He had brought glossy magazines and newspaper, a long-necked lighter, and—if it should come to it—lighter fluid (he kept this, shamefully, as a last resort, packed in his bag). They had drawn chairs and gathered the dry indoor logs to the hearth. Morgan had sat down with her book, neglected to open it, and watched as Edward constructed the box.

She'd allowed him to struggle. It was the most she could do. Edward created a square of logs then crisscrossed more on top. He jammed crumpled newspaper and magazine pages into the center and lit them with the lighter. At first, the flames would jump at the ink-damp paper and his eyes would widen with success and triumph, bravado that morphed into reasonable masculinity. He looked out of the adjacent window and, on cue, the first flakes of snow of the month began to fall. But soon, the pages were exhausted and the fire was gone, the wooden box not even smudged like the previously spent coal or the back of Morgan's hand or the top of her jeans or his will to continue. It was as if the whole world, suddenly, had become vulnerable. Or, that it always had been and was just now obvious.

"I think we have to cut them. Chop them. You know. The dry part is on the inside. We need kindling," she said.

"We don't have an axe."

"I guess not."

"You think there's one here?"

"I saw a shed out front but it was padlocked. Maybe around."

Edward stood and moved around the first floor of the barn, looking for an axe but really looking at the stacks of books. From the kitchen, he could see the back of Morgan's head, her hair pulled tightly into a bun, her arm near imperceptible but certainly circling at the elbow to maneuver her hand over her abdomen. There was no axe, only stacks of books.

Morgan jolted and brought her smudged hand to her belly, "She kicked."

Edward smiled at her, "That doesn't get old." She looked down at herself in amazement and breathed only when her body demanded.

He tried again at the fire, this time doubling the amount of wadded paper inside of the box. Again, the flames found purchase there, but not on the structural wood beyond the nucleus. The magazine-page smoke was purple and bulbous, thick the way it rose and barreled out of the fireplace into the room. It caused a blue translucence inside so that, in looking toward the kitchen, Edward could see the kitchen things as if through squinted touching eyelashes. "I don't think this is right," Morgan said.

"Of course it isn't," Edward replied, frustrated. His lone attempt at creating something as simple and meaningful as fire was becoming a failure. For all the cosmopolitan knowledge in the world he'd obtained while traveling the sinews of the city, all the accepted question marks of a diverse day, all the aptitude in raising Foster, all the strength of working and accepting digital currency into his bank account to digitally transfer it out to someone else's account each month—for all of that, he could not catch fire to wood. "Well," he said, "we're attending to it like good adults."

"I don't know if I should be breathing this," she said, raising her sleeve to cover her nose and mouth.

"Then don't."

He knew something was obstructing the chimney. As the pages burned down, the wood failing to catch, the smoke grew less viscous. Edward looked up into the chimney and saw a metal bar; he pushed it away from him and heard the metal reaction clinking above. Whatever smoke remained changed course from exiting into the room and drew up into the brick steeple. He turned to look out at Morgan; she was smiling at him, and for good effect—in an attempt at solidarity but also to ensure that this most recent find reestablished his footing in the practical world—she removed the sleeve from her face.

It was difficult to understand the beauty and ugliness of life, the horror and majesty, as they struck simultaneously.

"Will it survive?" she asked.

"I don't know."

Outside, the boy's footfalls thudded against the ground as he chased the dog into and out of the woods. The flame coiled cylindrically up from the log and had a blue-green vein in the middle of its transient shaft from the burning ink of the glossy magazine page Edward placed under the log to advance its hunger. He had put down the poker. To each other, they said little.

"We should have built the teepee," she said.

"I like the box. More sound."

"I just don't think it will catch this way."

"All we need are coals."

"Yes."

Morgan drummed her free fingers upon the book's hardcover, vibrating the words within. It may have been fledgling, but the fire was warm; she stretched her bare feet toward it and extended her toes out from one another. Between them, in the space they left at their separating, Edward could see the brightness of the fire. Its alien presence, a movement similar to that of its liquid antagonist but truly replicated nowhere else on Earth. Like her toes. He bent in and blew at the base of the hearth; the coals glowed and at the end of his exhale, nascent flames burst up with renewed energy. He sat back proudly and lifted the cover of his book, flirting with the title page, and letting it close back again.

"I think we got it," Morgan said.

"Yeah. It's going now." Edward never felt perfectly comfortable around a fire. He always thought it needed an extra log, always felt he couldn't leave it alone—for fear of it dying and for fear of it getting out of control (*his* dying). He'd overload a new fire with wood. He'd ruin the hearth with a bucket of water before bed. The fire, fueled by air and wood, seemingly came from nowhere but could quickly be everywhere and was like a book; it, too, feeding on paper, could come from anywhere—the words waiting to be collected, arranged. They existed, too, somewhere, and came from anywhere, and could be everywhere. Bound not by brick but by minds, they too burned.

"Since the election," she said, the others gathering wood outside, Morgan and Edward reasonably ignoring the carcinogenic breaths they took, the dog—just outside the window now—cocked rigid, nose taut, right forepaw bent at alert, spine ridgehair standing, pointing the arrow of its snout at a squirrel in the branches of a tree it could never climb, the boy crouched behind, willing it to hunt, and the rest of the world (before Morgan's comment) safely somewhere else, "nothing feels certain."

"No politics on vacation," Edward said.

"That sentence is rife with privilege."

Edward kept blowing at the base of the burning, instigating the fire, as if its height would represent his capacity. She continued, "He's a beast. I don't know how it could have happened. How people voted…it's as if he's inhuman." Her hand, again, in circles above her womb.

"Many humans aren't," Edward said. "Human, that is." He didn't mean to be cynical. He did not consider himself pessimistic. Just months ago, before the election, Edward would claim himself generally positive about the course of history, the direction of the country. He counted himself patriotic in as much as he was not prepared to allow injustice to become profligate American ideology (he was not prepared to go to war) but was comfortable in not having to face injustice directly, ever (he was not prepared to go to war). Such was his experience. He knew there was no such thing as America, that it was a fiction assuming land, where possession and description and national identity were as arbitrary as which powerful force signed which papers when. The Lenape. The British. The colonists. Now, with the boy outside, it was as if the world, in all of its border cleaving, had just become vulnerable. He knew this wasn't so. Everything always, ultimately, was.

"What will we do?" Morgan asked.

"Fight. Comply. I don't know. Where we are will dictate what we do."

"Where we are?"

"In the social order."

Morgan thought about this. The day after the election, in the rawness of it, the wound of it, the city was intolerable. She called Edward, hoping for some form of allegiance, and they'd agreed to look for some place outside of the city, some distant wilderness in which to retreat for a while. They found the barn. It was available

January. "Where are we in the social order?" she asked with as much enthusiasm as was necessary to reveal she didn't want to ask.

"Near the place where we can be outraged then contrite then patient enough to wait four years."

"The privilege, again."

"I don't know what else to say."

"I know."

"It sounds awful," she said.

"It is. We are."

"What about the children?"

"One day, they'll vote for beasts, too."

"I've never known you to be so sardonic. In college, you were the only white guy who pestered the Black Student Union for membership."

"That was wrong of me."

"But you wanted it for good reason."

"Did I? Or was I just insisting that I wasn't a white supremacist?"

"And now?"

"Now, everyone I walk by I distrust. Did they vote for him? Did my mother? Have we become a nation of solipsists stuck in the subjective?" Edward paused. "I wonder, sometimes, if we are doomed as a species. You know? Doomed to destroy ourselves in some biological, evolutionary way. Like we are biologically programmed to self-destruct every so often. For every hundred of us, only one seems intelligent. Human civilization proves itself endlessly and only capable of burning itself to nothing. We're Rome and the Soviet Union now. It's our turn."

"But the children," Morgan said. His rhetoric, so confused, so convoluted, so unlike the Edward of college, the Edward of even two months ago, frightened her.

"I know."

The snow came more forcefully now. Edward could see play in the dotted footprints of dog and boy scourging through the landscape outside of the window. Wyle and Em would be coming in soon, arms full of fuel. If she looked around just right, the barn's interior could provide enough illusion for her to believe herself home, believe herself in someone else's home, in another place, another land, not country or kingdom so much as environment, where the social structures ceded to mountains, where geography was no match for geology, the Earth just as it is and was and would be again regardless of human interaction. She thought it arrogant for people to be concerned about the Earth when considering global warming; they were only concerned about themselves—the Earth would be fine without us. She thought it arrogant that there were such words as *left* and *right* and *liberal* and *conservative* when these things were just inventions to justify morality and skim off the notion that such discourse ignored the fact that people's bodies—the physical entities of humanity—were being hurt. She thought herself arrogant to look at a barn interior and presume, even if it was a moment, that she was outside of it. That she could run: away, to the wild, to her thoughts, to her womb, to Canada.

Since college, Edward and Morgan hadn't spoken often. They lived in the same city but it was a big city and they had big lives. And every time, when round a circle, the finish is the start; and what that means is time thrusts through the universe, unstoppable, relentless, savage; barreling like a boy but with no trees to stop it, no lakes to swim through.

"It says it's just beyond that ridge," he said.
"What will it be?"
"I don't know."
"Like a cabin?"
"I don't know."
They'd gone sixteen miles and the weight of the packs dug their boots more deeply into the blisters of their heels. The spring water, clean and filtered into canteens, tasted like nothing and the wood-silence (full of noise) was balm: the snake rattle a disconcerting comfort, the jay's squawk an ugly pleasure. The trail, white-blazed, cut through the woods, trampled as it was with the trudging of previous hikers, which matted the earth in a darker, somehow richer brown and led infinitely and needed no paint blaze for direction. It's no wilder than the city, he thought, as if surprised.

They had armed themselves against antagonism. One car was parked at the terminus; the other, at the head. Their gear and provisions enough to last twice as long. New laces. The map. A hatchet, just in case. Its weight ever-bouncing against his hip enough evidence to suggest he was no Hawkeye, no Crusoe, no Jack London. How his literature class that semester was failing him.

She watched him ahead as they hiked. Sometimes they would separate a good distance, beyond voice call, before she'd blow the whistle he gave her for such occasions and he'd wait for her to arrive. He was long-legged, quick footed. He was designed to move at that rate; anything less would have been more exhausting than to have run. In class, he asked if she actually finished all of the assigned novels. He read at the pace he hiked; to have waited for her at each whistle call of a chapter's end would mean he'd be as little prepared for the final exam as she. She felt of the trail as she did the canon: the weight, the unkempt hair, the sweat-slick skin—all as tiresome as was the arbitrary appreciation of value, the vague distinction of that which was "literary," the need to leave their world for the world of wood, out there and in there (forests and books). He led her to both. To enrollment and to the trail. And even though it made tender the soil of her singularity, her own identity, the insistence that she was and could be an essential organism all unto herself, she went because he wanted her there.

"There," he said.

The shelter was a lean-to in a clearing into which the trail fed and out of which the trail continued. It was three walls, a floor, and a roof. On the map of this section, he had circled the triangle that marked this shelter as their halfway point, their stop, where they would spend the night in a wild that was tamed by the insistence that it was somehow outside of the rest of the world that had grown up around it. He was unsure that they would find it but when the trail proved itself to be almost ruler-straight in its design, he became more sure that the shelter would present itself at the appropriate time, when the miles receded to the map triangle that showed what previous people already knew. He unrolled his sleeping bag in the open mouth of the lean-to and took out a book. Lying with his head toward what was left of the sun, he opened it to read, his back against the planks of the building, his head just at the lip of the opening that was the threshold of the wilderness, his temporary retreat to an enclosure no less dignified than if they'd checked into a motel. She prepared a dinner that dissolved any final illusion of rusticity by boiling water on a gas-powered stove and pouring it into pre-designed, self-contained bags of freeze-dried food—lasagna. They ate it with dinner forks from her apartment then prepared for sundown.

It came. The first descent, beyond the trees and the ridge that concealed the mountains' peaks (she always imagined the singular spire pointing from the mountain's top, the conical image of a mountain that became a prototype for all mountains; what the ridge showed her was a continued peak, sharp and awkward because it was the highest elevation, abounding over everything, but there was no point, no pointing, no conical, snow-capped height that said *mountain* and showed her she was there). When the sky muted into pre-dusk, he closed his book and let out an exhale, turning to his stomach to look out into the woods, to see the shades darken as they came, so subtly it was as if every single hue was the only one in which he'd ever lived. The shadows of all things stretched into one another, filling the gaps of ground like liquid; it became cold. It occurred to him that he hadn't heard from her since they'd finished dinner and so looked over to where she was sitting on a wide tree stump, looking out into the forest from which they'd come. He asked if she was okay and received no response. He noticed her drawn into herself beyond what the cold called for.

In truth, she was horrified of the impending darkness, that which came slowly but just as forcefully. She could not fathom the prospect of sleeping exposed, in the lean-to, in a sleeping bag with nothing separating her from the outside. It was as if she was to sleep on a stage where the audience, beyond the fourth wall, could applaud or scorn her without the protection of curtain or screen. There was nothing typically or prejudicially feminine about it; she wasn't scared of bugs or being eaten or whatever it was out there that she couldn't see. What frightened her was being in the lean-to with him, in a bag but close, for the first time, but open to the outside world as if he could up and leave it at will or that someone could come and take him up the trail without her. What frightened her was the prospect of her reality, of chance as it presented itself, of what happens when people connect. She, like every single organism around, wanted that connection, but also feared it. Feared knowing what it might mean if on the other side of the ellipses, at sunup, they left the lean-to just as they'd entered it.

He little knew how to react to his own understanding of her wanting. Dawns and dusks: the important, pensive times of light, suns at horizons, were not meant for understanding. Only thinking. Night in the woods meant nothing. He shouldn't have come. He shouldn't have asked. In the dark, one could only hope for unconsciousness to come and there, after a day of exhausting work, it refused. The faster to the abyss the faster to sunrise, to breakfast and movement and sight. He zipped his bag and turned toward the lean-to wall. When she entered, zipped in too, he allowed the solid wood below to numb his side, unwilling as he was to turn toward her. Her body didn't move but something in her did. He couldn't give her anything.

Perhaps he entertained it because it brought him confidence, or cemented his arrogance, or clutched to his need; but what she felt for him—endlessly known in glances over the top edges of books—he did not feel for her.

Still, and always, he cared for their friendship, their connection. "Did you look up?" he asked.

She let breaths pass before she answered him. They were only as far away as a body, as their bodies, but she had no idea what he'd meant or how to answer or what to say or how to repair the chasm or how to create gravity between heavenly bodies. On campus, when he'd finished a chapter from the syllabus and said to her, "Two-day trek?" she'd replied then the same way she replied now, "What?"

"The stars," he said. "No light blindness, like in the city. We can see everything."

She turned her attention from his back to the sky beyond the roof of the lean-to and, yes, they were impossibly there. Stars that replicated the few she could see from a dark alley in the city, betraying that there were far more than she'd ever known, than she ever could know. They were endless, connected by the white translucent web of the galaxy, speckled with sublimity, an infinity of ellipses connecting everything that was known and unknown and beyond the concept of knowing; they connected them only and all as a part of the every them, so that it was impossible to separate one body from another. They could never be separate, space dust as they were, one gaseous explosion that stretched them, but kept them together endlessly.

"Periods used to worry me," he said. "The idea of the final, full stop. But if you put three together, you connect to the next. And if you see animal eyes out there tonight, they are just more stars, dotting in twos, connecting."

She gathered what was compact of her in the bag and let it loose in relaxation, "Promise me," she said, "if things ever get really bad, we'll find a cabin to retreat to."

The barn was warm and by then Wyle, Em, and Foster had entered with the dog, put all the wood they could carry by the hearth, complemented the construction of the fire, and set about doing their own things around the barn. As the winter warranted, the day had shrunk to nothing at too early an hour, leaving them in an obscure world before dinnertime and with near no stimulus. It should have been fine: away from the city and its endless goading, attentions diverted to every corner, every space; each typical walk showing something different as if the city itself was changing between strolls, and here—the fire should have been enough. Family and fidelity. The escape. But between the two chairs was the apex of elasticity, the endpoint beyond which nothing could stretch, a tautness vulnerable to micro-tear before total collapse. What affection Morgan had felt for Edward in college had matured into a stoic blandness, encased as it was in their distant friendship, and prosaic as it had to be in their new lives with others. Back, in the world beyond the barn, it was as if someone was chiseling at the anchor of a hold that kept the Earth in orbit and revolution; and inside something similar picked at the meeting points of little worlds. When lives go on, sometimes the spaces between them fill with nothing.

No books were read.

"Have you decided what you're going to name her?" Edward asked.

"Yes. But Wyle and I have decided not to tell anyone."

Micro-tear.

A chopping resonated from Em's wrist through the viscera of zucchini and Foster, ever-vigilant to unspoken energy, came up to his father. His sweater harbored things from the woods, leaves and twigs that betrayed a rolling around, which betrayed a need for little else. "Hadley's eyes glowed," he said.

"Where?"

"In the woods."

"What do you think of that?"

"It's okay."

"Do you know why they do that?" Edward asked, one eye on the fire.

"No."

"Think."

"I can't."

"So you'll always know where she is, Foster. Like how we talked about how sailors used the stars to know where they were. Hadley's eyes tell you where she is."

"I think I'll go help mom," Foster said, galloping away to the kitchen as if Edward's comment fleeted up the flue. Hadley's head rose as Foster rushed by and Edward noticed Foster look back at her eyes. Made sure she was there.

There was no television and no radio and no service and so there was no telling what was happening out there in the world. The end of January usually meant little more than the beginning of February but this year the guilt they all felt in not paying attention to the world could be muted for the moment. It was a weakness, but cowering was as much a defense as biting.

"Why did you and Em name him Foster?" Morgan asked.

"Because it's what we're supposed to do with them," Edward responded. "His name reminds us."

The coals glowed elegantly in the magic that they were and the fresh logs around were enough to keep that warmth breathing into the evening and dinner would be prepared soon for them to sit around the adjacent table as a group, a clandestine refuge against enmity and precipitation and threatening eyes and falling stars and anything a hand on a book could do to anything that moved against the essence of what they were. It was a counterfeit comfort bestowed upon them because they had the opportunity to escape; but it was essential to understand that their moment, regardless of how momentous, was still theirs and that they should live it because it was theirs to live and in another moment it would be gone, which is the sequence that results similarly for everyone.

"Mariposa," Morgan said, looking not at the fire but at its flames reflecting in Edward's glowing eyes. "The name."

Atoms are always and essentially rushing apart. Things break and things are built. Edward picked up three pieces of coal he'd removed from the fireplace earlier and placed them between himself and Morgan in a line. They sat back, opened their books, and read.

US VS

"This is a dangerous place," Shirley said, as they passed under the cage-cloistered walkway. There, tigers could prowl the grounds from one end to another, safely behind links of chain that were woven small but not small enough to guard against children's fingers. "It has the illusion of safety, but you have to be careful."

Lawrence, her son—who went by Laurie—tripped over his toddler steps and had to be righted by his vigilant mother. "Very careful," she concluded. Shirley wasn't enthusiastic about zoos; she maintained a quasi-self-righteous theory that the act of holding animals in captivity committed some vague, menial sin against nature, despite her husband's assertion that they were domesticated, and thus, useless in the wild. "It is one of civilization's greatest accomplishments," he opined, maybe bored but certainly genuine in wanting to provide Laurie with all of the benefits of the social institutions of cities: like children's museums and zoos and public transportation, "that we can have a place where children and wild animals can..." he trailed off.

In the end, Shirley's imagination—Laurie, now a zoologist at a foreign university researching the humane, ethical treatment of zoo animals, redeemer of his mother's trespasses—and the constant need to find occupying things for small children won out, and the family rode the train to the zoo's entrance, where Laurie exclaimed giddily at the prospects ahead.

From the train car, Shirley felt both knighted and nicked on the neck.

She was a schoolteacher and an atheist, despite once taking a college course called *Biblical and Classical Literature* and finding perfection in Jesus's central thesis of compassion. Her charge, in raising Laurie, was to help foster an agent of altruism—a person who knew the value of living for others. Her husband was a poet (not famous, but celebrated enough for an income based on speaking engagements) so he thought, and often spoke, in annoying idioms that were meant as social criticisms but fell as simple attempts at poignancy. In response to the sight of a family who'd left their SUV with bags of fast food for the gates of the zoo, he offered, "Casino America: sadly sitting at slots." Shirley had made sure there were enough cloth diapers for the day.

Past the caged tiger-walkway, past the cashier windows where the families paid the exuberant entrance fees—Shirley: "How ridiculous that each member of the family must buy a ticket, even the child"; her husband: "It feeds your dear deer, dear."—past the food court where dropped ice cream globes melted on the ground in pools of their own color, past extraneous business men in everyday business suits ("Their casual ties are casualties," [guess who]) past the wailing and chirping of all the other children—past it all, the family wandered in the lovely indecisiveness of places that demanded no linear progress. Laurie was willed each way, and it brought Shirley no little joy that her son magnetized to the exhibits; there was a certain childish beauty in the innocent way he felt a kinship with the animal kingdom.

Shirley and her husband lived by tenets that they hoped to pass along to Laurie:

—all people are of a collective (in the Buddhist tradition) and so helping another is helping yourself.

—a dedication to truth and beauty (in the Romantic tradition) triumphs over a lust for wealth and power.

—self-reliance (in the Transcendentalist tradition) is the highest virtue to which one can aspire.

—it is more important to live passionately than to live conformitively (in the etymological tradition).

—education and labor (in the colonial American tradition) are the ways to freedom.

and—kindness is as essential as cleanliness.

They were in no way flawless in achieving these designs, nor were they faultless in their attempts. They encountered the world in their particular way, were forced to react to it, and so built a structure that seemed to best fit their souls.

They were educated in universities.

They donated to charities.

They voted Democrat (but always flirted Independent) in the primaries.

They collected books, rarities.

But clandestinely enjoyed sitcoms on the TV.

They were good, dangerous, American people.

The zoo organized the animal exhibits by close proximities of species: the reptile house, for instance, was close to the aviary, perhaps owning to the theory that birds evolved from dinosaurs and crocodiles looked like dinosaurs; or, maybe, in the event of some unfortunate apocalypse, the reptiles could eat the birds before they flew away to tell other civilizations how badly we'd screwed up.

Laurie was particularly fond of the polar bear house, where a glass wall was half privy to the underwater indulgences of the bears and half showed their more static shore-bound lives. The watermark, high above Laurie's own head, betrayed to the adults that the bears were largely disinterested—in anything. Underwater, where the children could see them twirl and hunt for imaginary prey, the bears seemed free, happy, unaware that they were far from their namesake poles. In this way, the parents could sustain the fantasies they told their children.

"It's the summer. It just feels wrong," Shirley said to her husband, while Laurie banged on the *Do Not Bang* sign.

"It's air conditioned," her husband said. "They live better than we do."

The bears did, Shirley had to admit, seem pretty pleased with themselves.

Along the glass wall lined children of various ages, but they all shared one commonality: their palms against the glass, their fingertips leaving prints to be sprayed and wiped by the evening cleaning crew. The water's blue was unnatural, colored by the painted underwater landscape, but it provided a perfect background for the whiteness of the bears. Laurie banged in the domino unison of the other kids banging, each slapping down the line to get the attention of the bear that, if he heard, pretended not to, and instead, floated down to the bottom—facing away—as if to drown himself. Shirley watched with anticipation, hoping he'd kick the ground and surface; but as time passed, she wondered what the problem was; was the bear truly, finally giving in, through with the world of cages and banging children?

"He's not going to make it!" she exclaimed, a little too loudly. The other mingling, agitated parents looked over. Her husband touched her arm, noticed something else, and withdrew it. "He's going to drown himself!"

"What?" her husband asked.

"The bear, look!"

"The bear?"

"Yes, look. The bear. It's sunk. It doesn't want to come back up."

By this point the panic of the frantic woman had captured the attention of all of those in the room who could see above the waterline. There was some muted laughter; others watched with a perfunctory look of concern. Still others were drawn away in ennui-reverie by the next adjacent sound.

"Shirley, honey," her husband said. "Surely, Shirley, the bear is fine. He can bear it, even if bare, just by living his barely bear life…"

"Oh Jesus, stop," Shirley interrupted, and went hurriedly to the glass, displacing two children in route. She banged on the glass. "Bear!" she exclaimed. "Bear, bear!"

As if on cue, as if it was a setup by the zookeepers—this one-act, once-an-hour show—the polar bear looked over its shoulder briefly at Shirley, kicked the floor, surfaced, climbed onto a stone ledge, ambled over to a corner, and went to sleep.

A staff member walked over, "Please don't bang on the glass, ma'am."

In the absence of the bear, the children scattered around the room. The zoo's staff predicted such animal downtime and so left for the children an array of occupying amusements.

Laurie grabbed such an amusement: a piece of a puzzle. It wasn't a table puzzle piece but a large wooden block with barely enough distinction to separate it from its peers. Shirley watched from a darkened corner of the room, embarrassed at herself for the histrionics and marveled at how children could entertain themselves with such unimportant things, such common smallnesses.

Another boy—who was almost indistinguishable from Laurie save for his clothing (decidedly, it was more haggard) and who was actually (though Shirley didn't realize it) part of the family who'd exited their SUV with the fast food earlier—walked up to Laurie and snatched the puzzle piece out of his hand. Shirley's instinct was to move forward, to chide the little colonizer and return the rightful prize to her son, but she resisted in part because she was currently practicing the brutal parental object of allowing her son to react independently to the challenges of the world and partly because of what Laurie did next. Her little boy bent to the ground, picked up another puzzle piece, and offered it to the child who'd stolen the first. It was a benevolent act, a moment of pure kindness, which prided Shirley so much that she reached out to her husband to point it out—but he was reading a plaque on a nearby wall that didn't provide information about polar bears but rather the most prudent evacuation points in case of fire (where would the bears go?). The other little boy grabbed at Laurie's proffered gift—a little violently, Shirley thought—and, with it, returned to his parents. Laurie looked on with the same bewildered face he seemed to reserve for the exhibits.

Shirley looked from the other toddler to his parents and exhaled an audible sigh of exasperation so loud that it seemed stage-acted: for the back row. She began to do what she promised herself at the moment of Laurie's conception that she would never do: she began judging the parents. Clearly, they hadn't taught *their* little boy any manners. Certainly, he'd grow up to be some capitalist who thought it ethical—in the way that corporations were granted the legal rights of living humans—to slit the throats of his neighbors in order to buy a bigger boat. Obviously they felt their little harem more special, unique, important than any other, and so protected their cloister with the personal morality of ignoring the privileges they'd been born with in favor of a meritocratic belief in their evolved greatness. Shirley thought all of these things in the fraction of a second in which she registered the boy's parents, before her eyes could really adjust to what they looked like.

The mother wore a cross necklace the size of a billboard *t* and the length of a rosary and the father was wrapped in the patriotic gluttony of antagonistic flags: the flag of The United States contorted into a bandanna around his head and the flag of the Confederate States stretching across his broad chest with a caricature eagle below it that flexed an alien arm into a discomforting biceps. At the father's hip was a revolver. He looked like a man who would love the word *suffocate*. The mother looked down with approval at her returned son and announced, "You got two!" In so saying this, she glanced over at Shirley.

Shirley didn't think. She trudged over to the couple and demanded, "Do you know your son stole those, those, whatevers from my son?"

"What?" the mother asked.

"Your son. Your boy. He stole those, those *pieces* from my son, right over there." Shirley pointed back to Laurie, who was sitting on a bench in the middle of the room, watching the blue underwater for the return of the bear.

"Hank, Jr.? He didn't steal nothin'."

"He did," Shirley reminded. "From right over there. He took those pieces from Laurie and I think he should give them back."

"Laurie?" the father asked, smirking. Shirley had been through this before. "You named your son Laurie?"

"Yes. No. Listen. Is your, is Hank *Junior* going to give the pieces back to Laur…to my son or what?" Shirley's husband had, somehow, noticed the second commotion his wife was making in the polar bear house and—out of the obligatory bravado of masculine expectation—slowly trudged over to stand beside his wife. He noticed two things: the tension in the space and his antagonist's gun.

"It becomes apparent to a parent," he started, and Shirley's blood pressure moved toward stroke, "that this sort of thing causes pauses in how we should consider some burdens that don't have to be burdensome." All members of the scene looked at him.

"What the hell did he just say?" the other father asked.

"I don't know," Shirley responded. "Listen, have Hank here, Hank *Junior* here, you're Hank, Hank *Senior*, I gather…have him give my son back his puzzle pieces."

"Listen lady," the other mother said, "I don't know what you're talking about, but I suggest you go on your own way."

"What?" Shirley asked, nodding to the hip of the other husband, "Is he going to shoot me?"

Everyone looked at her quietly. "Let me guess," Shirley continued, "that's for your protection. The zoo animals might get too rowdy. There might be a stampede."

Shirley heard her husband whisper to himself, "*Evolve… revolver…re-evolve…*"

The other mother put one hand on her husband's shoulder and the other on the shoulder of her son; the boy put both puzzle pieces to the floor as the mother guided the three of them out of the polar bear house. Shirley stood in the crowd, again reduced to anonymity in the tumult's wake—lucky for the expedience with which people rush chaos back into normalcy.

"They vote tyrants into the White House," she said, "I bet."

The giraffes' black tongues licked mucus spikes into unwitting spectators' heads.

The apes were grabby for pocketbooks and bottoms.

The fish stared endlessly out into the airy world, wondering what all the people breathed.

Flamingos balanced.

Snakes tongue-taunted.

The tortoises held the world.

The zoo was a place of magic for Laurie, who, not understanding anything of the structure or system, could ignorantly revel in the collection of these things the Earth contained. To the child, it was a cosmopolitan utopia (though he didn't know the phrase) where all things co-existed simultaneously and without the need or desire to harm one another. He couldn't see the fences as cages.

Shirley hadn't thought of it—as interested as she was in the criminality of cages—but the zoo, then, was, ultimately, unmistakably, a ferocious lie.

"I'm a good person," she thought to herself, unable to get the other family from the polar bear house out of her mind. She replayed the events to herself and, as they began to blur with infidelity, she couldn't decipher what she had said in contrast to what she wished she would have said.

"I'm a good person," she thought again, absent to her surroundings, as if repeating the mantra would actualize what had quickly become dubious. Was she? It was her tendency to remember her past with herself as the villain; all of her memories contained at least some aspect of how she fumbled through a conversation or situation, how she'd made the wrong choice or behaved deplorably. It was, as if, in fading into sleep, she had failed to realize the self she imagined as she emerged from dreaming earlier that morning. "I'm a good person," she thought. "*He* was the one with the oxymoronic T-shirt/bandanna combo. The pair of them, with a cross and a gun. Turn the other cheek then put a hole through someone else's. *Their* fast food. *Their* pro-life. *Their* Second Amendment. All force-fed with a too-big spoon, all breathed in through a straw. *I'm* the good person here. Laurie, *he's* the good boy. *We* care about life even *after* the womb. *We* know what ills guns cultivate in society. *We*, damn it, *we* think everyone should have healthcare, right? I mean, I went to college! That's it," she thought. "They didn't go to college, surely. Or, if they did, it was in Texas or something."

But no amount of rationalizing, of progressing through the developed and sustained machinations of subjective cultural divides, could prevent Shirley from thinking she did something wrong in the polar bear house, and it ate at her—chewed with molars—until she felt swallowed.

A fiery swath of dusk sunlight draped across the path they walked, toward the aviary, where a small crowd had gathered to peer through the fences. When they approached, it became apparent to Shirley that the crowd was thick enough to restrict proper viewing, no matter how one positioned oneself at the fringes of the focus or in-between the tallest people who seemingly always got places in front. Her husband offered to lift Laurie onto his shoulders but the idea couldn't materialize enough as Laurie was swallowed up by the shifting legs of adults. Shirley could see Laurie if she tottered for a sightline through the crowd, and so felt no real alarm. She stood, somewhere near the back, with her hands in her pockets, and tried to look at whatever had drawn the crowd.

There were signs that asked visitors to not climb the fencing, but there was a row of elevated children with toes in the diamonds of links and hands grasped onto wire. For the parents behind, perhaps because they'd grown older, enthusiasm had been relinquished to an indifference that welded to normalcy. Like on airplanes, Shirley thought, where the safety instructions of flight attendants were no longer watched because flying was rote and all the adults could ignore the miracle of a machine that flew. And anyway, what good were oxygen masks when a four-hundred ton cylinder of fuel fell from the clouds?

Shirley caught a glimpse within the fences. The birds lifted in streams and released down in circles, negotiating their enclosure with a confidence that proved they knew no sky. They were beautiful. Shirley was as engrossed as the rest of the crowd as the birds glided, their enormous wingspans and plumage open in a grace that slowed her heart rate. Even her husband had lost his verbosity; he stood quietly with his lips just separated, breathing shallowly and watching.

There were two of them, and though it seemed they were unaware of one another, it was clear that their flight was choreographed: their movements were dependent upon the circuit of the other.

The birds perched upon a faux-tree branch molded and painted to look like wood and Shirley took the opportunity to walk over to the worn, unattended plaque that vainly tried to educate: *Haliaeetus leucocephalus*. The bald eagle. Of course, Shirley thought, the most beautiful animal in the zoo would be a bald eagle. Its majesty preceded even it. The birds' talons, wrapped around the perch, were as sharp and ominous as their beaks, and Shirley looked away whenever one of the yellow eyes seemed to focus on her. It was an intimidating bird— the way its beauty and menace converged in one organism. It was hard to look at, but she wanted to touch it.

The perched eagles didn't provide as much excitement for the impatient crowd, whose diminished attention span caught wind of a mewing shrew nearby and so began to disperse in its direction. Even

Shirley's husband had re-pursed his lips, and in noticing the flight of the aggregate, began working the gears of his ingenious, belabored brain, "The crowd crowed, then, cowards, they cowered."

Laurie remained at the fence, his toes jutted into links, his little hands grasped tight around the fencing, and his body pulled in. His nose squarely inside a diamond, his eyes trained on the eagles, Laurie regarded them with a natural kindness. Next to him, in the exact same posture, was Hank, Jr.

Then Shirley noticed, the crowd thinned to straggling, that the *other* couple, the polar-bear-house couple, Hank, Jr.'s parents, were there, too. The still-life portrait: two toddlers grasped against a chain-link fence, their spectrum-distant parents a parentheses on either side, all in the company of staring eagles enclosed in a city zoo. "Write *that* poem, honey" Shirley telepathically, chidingly, challenged her husband. By the look on his face, he already had been.

The two toddlers ignored one another in the presence of the birds; the two couples ignored each other in the chasm that lay between them: the barrenness between their beliefs and the momentary altercation of their immediate past. They were as far away as land between two distant coasts and as near as the shoulder width of two side-by-side children. Shirley felt the universal discomfort of a limb dangling over the edge of a bed; out of sight, the endless, carnivorous species below.

No one noticed that the birds hadn't taken off again. No one noticed that, in their neglect, the birds were undernourished, unkempt. No one noticed that, in concentrating so hard to avoid one another, something was wrong. So no one called for the attention of a zookeeper. No one noticed that keeping birds in cages violated a fundamental design of nature. No one noticed the agony of their trespass against those beautiful things. No one noticed that, its beak tipped toward chest plumage, one of the eagles had died. The tongue had slithered out lazily, its death ignoble; even its mate didn't seem to mind. No one noticed what they, in their reproach, did to it.

The dusk light moved to vanish. Laurie turned from the cage and returned to his parents. Finally, Shirley thought, we can leave this place—and go home.

The Anthologist of Ideas

His teeth were the white of professional intervention and, as he smiled at us, I felt implored to turn away. The tweed and corduroy blazers of my colleagues vibrated audibly with restless discomfort and our beard lengths (those of us with the capacity) seemed to inch longer, furtive in competition against one another's growth. I exhaled openly, aggrieved; it was to be a long morning that led into an even longer afternoon. Why did we have to be so much the same?

Upon arrival into the wide room with old stone walls and a wooden circular table—around which we had positioned ourselves and practiced the pleasantries of deep culture—he introduced himself only as Mr. A, the coyness of it in no way as precocious and casual as I thought he'd hoped, and refused to sit. Rather, he revolved around the table, making eye contact with each of us in circuit, those teeth stabbing light into my eyes.

We were, ostensibly, called there—to that university, that prestigious place in England, where the buildings allowed for the droughts of castles—from our corners of the world, with the promise of exploring the deepest mysteries of mankind, the quintessential question mark of the human condition. The email we received, with the formal business letterhead perfunctory on stationary but somehow odd on a screen, told of all expenses paid, a large stipend, and most drawingly, flattered with the idea that (in italics) *we* were the greatest minds alive in the world today. I thought it was spam, at first. Our Departments had been notified and sabbaticals were preemptively arranged for the symposium. How could we not?

The project, our object: a compilation of the professorate from varied disciplines, accomplished in our individual ways, to sit in a communal space for one week and hash out the answer to the questions riddled through by all philosophy, religion, art, and thought throughout time. The *why* of our lives. That's it.

I was appropriately skeptical. Why did this renowned university, the one that maintains the history of English language, call together such minds for the most pretentious of affairs? More importantly, I left my own campus in the US with no belief whatsoever that it could be done, that anyone could ever do it, that the central notion of the mystery of the human condition was that it *was* a mystery and if we found it, the paradox would be that we would no longer be human. Still, my ego and the promise of posh lodgings (and who *doesn't* need a vacation?) put me on the plane, got me to that room, and had me realize the conformity of the "minds" positioned so imposterly around the table.

"You'll have all of the support and resources of the university," Mr. A concluded in describing our task. I noticed he didn't have a British accent. "Anything you need. Money is no object here."

"Then," said a man with grey cascades of hair slinging from the flaked flesh baldness of scalp, "what *is* the object? This is what I cannot understand. Why set out on an adventure where the destination is a fabricated insecurity shared by our collective unconscious?"

Ah, so *he* was the Psychology prof.

"A fair question," Mr. A responded; and here, here's where he got us, "You ever miss…you ever feel nostalgic about the pursuit of knowledge? The unabashed need of it? You ever stop to think in all of your research, all of your thinking, all of your creation, that something is lost today? That in our modern world, academia has become a process, a banal thing, bereft of its true intentions and imagination? You ever wish you could just think openly without the stress and expectation surrounding it? Even if we fail, you ever just wish you could try again?" I could tell he wasn't a professor. A dean, maybe. "The complete brain is a diverse brain. We'll need both concrete and imaginative thinking."

We all had coffee.

We'd all be drunk later.

Uppers and downers. The masters of the world.

We were teachers, in the flexible sense.

Most of us didn't interact much with students; we couldn't tell a classroom from a bathroom, a class from a bath. Our home universities were just spaces we filled with our egos by filling the informed world with more information. Students were rocks around which our streams had to flow—cold as rocks, smart as rocks. Their awkward bodies retarded my progress in the hallways, blocked access to my office door, distracted me from my next Great American Novel—I did not have time for their corporate endeavors, their education for a job. I was on perpetual release time (all of us at the round table were): the resident novelist English Professor. I was tenured.

So I suppose *my* job in all of this was to condense what literary texts as artifacts of human thought suggested about our pointless existence. The rub was, I was a writer, not a professor of literature, which meant I didn't read a lot of books; I never taught books. My job was to sit at my desk, write prose, delete prose, write prose, delete it, and carry on this way until my agent demanded a draft and I turned in whatever was left over from the slaughter. My name had become enough a marketing tool for them to publish whatever. I didn't know how to write; I knew what people wanted to read. The awards came tumbling in. If I ever found myself in a classroom, all I did was collect student writing, cross off every paragraph with egregious red Xs (it was better if the ballpoint slit the page), and pretend I was sitting with a bunch of laureates. But to hell with it: if Mr. A wanted some ad hoc *raison d'etre* for his troubles, he'd have it. He *was* paying for it.

The campus was ethereal. My university was obsessed with glass-curtained buildings housing plastic furniture; this place grew like stone waves splashing their rock droplets about the sky. The Green was a manicured checkerboard. The spires, incisors. When I arrived from the train, I walked through the town toward the university. The way wasn't difficult. It was apparent in the flow of humanity, in the way the place was built upon this central fulcrum where everyone seemed to lean as if orbiting in the conflicting currents of a maelstrom, where the campus was. I couldn't help but feel intimidated; the stone preceded me and it would outlast me. What was, after all, the difference between a mountain and a building made of stone? God-or-people-placed, rock was everlasting next to the flesh of man.

When I arrived, I was spotted immediately. They'd had a photo of me; they were on the lookout. I was shuttled into the round-table room—the last to arrive—before I could fully understand the scope of the place. There, amidst the conformity of our statures, my colleagues and I were abandoned by Mr. A, and a strange thing happened: those so naturally tasked with being the lighthouses of a room decided not to be beacons. We were awkwardly silent, each not wanting to be the first fool. Our shared language here, obligatorily, was English, but not all of us spoke it as a first language. There were mental translations to make; there was typical human shyness; there was a need to not seem the knave in a stage play full of wizards.

"Hawking suggests, 'The eventual goal of science is to provide a single theory that describes the whole universe,'" said a young man with only the first of grey sprouts in his beard. "Reginald Q. Dean," he added. Ph.D. Physics. Full Professor at Cambridge. Nobel Prize, twice, for his research on time's variance of something something something.

"Art has the same goal." This from a woman shivering despite her endless clothing; she seemed lost in textile, desperate in a hurricane of cloth, somehow still cold. "Athena B. Henry. Art. Austin Community College." Everyone looked up. The profs scoffed. "I know," she said.

Dean looked at her like an exotic sexual object—fetishizing the aboriginal. "Art and science the same effort," he said, flirting. Metaphysical eyebrow-raising. Allegorical leg-patting.

"Divorced in the university," Henry responded, game, "but wedded to the same effort: an unending journey of answering questions." Co-ed perversion. Pub fumbling. I couldn't believe this was how we'd begun.

"I know everyone wants me to say something about sex," the man who'd questioned Mr. A, the psychology professor, said. Abrams T. Wiley. Full Professor of Psychology. Goethe University Frankfurt. Famous for his treatise on the development of the superego in the age of something something something. "But I won't." That's all he said.

It seemed apropos, in the wake of the preamble of bedding between Dean and Henry and the jibe of Wiley at the two, that we introduce ourselves. I began.

"Wilson R. Pock. Full Professor of English. *The* Ohio State University." National Book Award. Pulitzer, twice. Famous for novels about something something something.

"Gwendolyn O. Pierce. Mathematics. Full. McGill." Known for an important equation.

"Mustafa Y. Said, Ph. D. Full Professor of Sociology, University of Tehran." Celebrated ostensibly for a tome titled: *Guns and Muscles: A History of Power*.

"Bethany C. Nguyen. Theology and Religious Studies. Vietnam National University." Known for thinking about God.

"Philosophy. University of Michigan." Was I seeing things? Did he glare at me? Football antagonism, here?

"Your name?" I asked pointedly, just in case he did.

"Oh, uh. Spalding. Horatio L. Spalding." He was famous for thinking things.

"And I'm Eric X. Reed. Full Professor of Business Administration. University of Glasgow." For the life of me, I couldn't think of where I'd heard of him before.

So there we were. Nine of us. The best minds in Physics, Art, Psychology, Literature, Mathematics, Sociology, Theology, Philosophy, and Business: about to wander around in a slush of supposition, to undertake the most intolerable task of all time—substituting awe for truth.

That first day didn't include much more. There was some side discourse on university positions, the general merits of research, cattiness and careerism lined with some posturing, and surely some below-table calf-toeing; but we all agreed to meet the next day to sincerely begin our work. I could tell two things at our conclusion: 1) No one was taking the task very seriously; we were too involved with whatever project we were currently obsessed with to care, and 2) When discussions began, we were all going to take the task very seriously, if only to not be upstaged by one another, just in case this forum netted any real gain. They had banked on our egos.

We attempted to elect a facilitator to lead the discussion; we failed to do so.

In looking for a pub to alleviate myself from the agony of being in that room for a week, I walked to the very outskirts of town, right where the cobbled streets began ceding to the concrete of faster roads, to find a place far from the university. It, I reckoned, would also be far from my colleagues.

I entered and lo, they were all there. All except Dean (Physics) and Henry (Art), who were noticeably absent, unmistakably together, likely entwined as much in correlating atoms to aesthetics as they were with appendages. All there, of course. All walked the same route to the end of town to get away, only to find one another. I bowed to the futility of resisting fate and joined the small table in the corner, with re-purposed pew benches on either side, at which sat my colleagues. The corner, obligatory dark. The atmosphere, perfunctorily rank.

I ordered a pint.

We talked as best we could in the way of people not like us, who didn't think as deeply as us—trying against ourselves to insist we were anything but what we were. This was the way with everyone. I allowed my eyes to unfocus on the surface of the table, the woodgrain at first sharp, then diffuse.

I thought about how sad it was that I would have, at best, only forty or fifty autumns left. That I wasted so many before coming to the realization. It made the reason for life difficult to see, like flint spark in dense groves. I was a sailor in a submarine, missing rain, knowing I was inside of steel that was submerged in water, and such a capture made air above an excruciating abstraction. I was a metaphor mixer.

But poisoning brain cells with substances that confuse all importance and relegate everything to idolatry eventually tends to breed either vitriol or amnesty, and sometimes progeny after pugilism. In other words, we became a group of sort of ludicrous friends. This was marked by the preciousness of calling each other not by our names but by our disciplines. This was how, in England, I became known as English. Psych reminded us: "We'll have to let Art and Physics in on the game when we see them next."

"Wearing the same outfits," snarked Theo.

Busi (we'd even truncated full discipline names to nicknames) was the only one of us to remain reasonably quiet throughout the evening. I took a concentrated interest in him (what was a Humanities education, after all, if not to encumber the scholar with the tools of endless critical analysis?) and noticed he drank his beer with sips that suggested temperance: he would draw often from the glass but never consume much, as if he were being careful. He looked at us cautiously, studying us like the market he so adored. We were stock tickers parading through his conniving; perhaps I was being unfair.

But I followed him anyway.

What else was I going to do? I hadn't even checked in to my hotel (though I was told by representatives of the university that my things would be placed unmolested in my room) and was intoxicated enough to plot an adventure against this supposed nemesis by following him at an inconspicuous distance through the winding streets that were labyrinthine enough for such a mission. Though an impostor of a novelist, I had enough of the romanticism of literary intrigue left in me to do things like this as if I were following plot points in a second-rate mystery yarn. My deeper conscious knew that I was just bored, but my drink-fortified courage propelled me on, after Busi, across the cobbles of town.

It shocked me a little, when, after a time, we ended up back on campus. Busi snuck around stone pillars and across the shadowed paths in what seemed an ominous gait. Was I making this up? Could it be that I was taking this too far? Or did it seem something shifty was actually afoot? It was bizarre to think it, but my undeveloped intention of catching my perp red-handed in some sinister affair began to feel somehow legitimate. It was the tilt in his walk. The cautiousness in his head turning. His incessant littering of whatever candy wrappers he trailed after him like breadcrumbs. Busi was up to something and I would be the sleuth to sniff it out.

It would make a great book.

Or, one that would sell.

Busi entered a building through a wooden door and I counted an odd number of heartbeats before following. It opened to a hallway completely concealed in dark. Progress was nevertheless easy, despite the obscurity, as the walls were just beyond shoulder width. I made my way by finger feel in the only direction available, still unable to penetrate the blackness without even the pinprick of wicklight. There were turns and forks and I made the most do with intuition and faith, pushing along protected mainly by the belief that nothing could truly befall me there. I was no explorer, no spelunker, but a random trespasser on the hook for little more than a confused expression from a bored security guard. The fact of it emboldened me. But the passageways became colder and seemed endless. Those buildings, I knew, weren't eternal. They had perimeter walls. So I kept on, despite what seemed an unfortunate amount of time without action. How was it that I could continue to curve without egress? Worse, there was no sign of Busi, or anyone. In the way that adrenaline dries up to leave the heart beating on boring blood again, I became unreasonably sick with the thought that I was trapped in some medieval labyrinth designed by old minds with a bent toward contrived architecture. Coming from a campus obsessed with squares, where there were four corners to each building and fire exits at every one (no school wanted to be sued), I was thusly unequipped to find an outlet in such a knotted network. How would it be received that such a superiorly intelligent member of the literati died of starvation in the bowels of a building only because he didn't know that there, presumably, three sequential lefts from any one spot led to the outside, or some such key?

I did the only reasonable thing: I panicked. I ran. Still no light, still no people, I bounded down the halls an impotent juggernaut delirious with escape. There were noises from the other side of the stone walls. Scratches, rat screeches. Something(s) moving at my pace. No matter how reasonable, how intellectual, how rooted in the empirical mind one is: when in a dark, enclosed space with no clear exit and disconcerting sounds, one melodramatizes, slightly. I ran, screaming stupidly, against the curves of the hallways, flailing as if on fire. I had sobered considerably at this point and had lost all inertia in making this a literary adventure. I felt enclosed, coffin-clad, plagued by the stomach illness of an innocent inmate given a life sentence—a whole existence restricted. The thought, the very idea, that I could be trapped permanently with no will of my own, to cycle endlessly in the cold stone darkness of academia, brought up some of the remnants of my night through my esophagus and into my mouth; remarkably, I somehow wished for decorum, denied its egress, and swallowed.

What stalled me was losing my breath (the way the mind works: I promised a God I didn't believe in that if I survived, I'd take up exercise, price check a good treadmill). I sat. The sounds persisted and I thought they would drive me crazy, until, reaching my hands to the ground, I felt a small object. A crinkle. Paper. The unmistakable wrapping of a candy, doubtlessly littered there by Busi as he made a similar progress down this hallway. So he *had* come this way; I wasn't a wanton wanderer. The thought of it raised me, propelled me again. I rushed on, forgetting his real name, calling "Busi!" My voice rebounded to me, anxious, sounding deep like a profound echo, sounding like I was announcing to the world I was "busy," that I couldn't be burdened with stopping. The only reply was mine.

My heart hurt from the beating but I ran on, more quickly, windmilling my arms as if to open throttle to a new speed, scooping air—"busy" echoes and scratches in pursuit—the clapping of my feet on the stone ground, the stone walls at my shoulders, in the midst of a goddamn tunnel (sorry, I'll exercise, I promise), a cave, a rock gauntlet, a shut chute, gravel casket, corridor of boulder—I will *quit* writing this instant, retire, age away—running because that's what there was to do (the existential dread of it: the running all we can do, the forward progress of our train tracks into a tunnel we'd never elect to enter) and running running running…

Into a door. Of course there would be a door. Of course that was how it would end. It was metal and had the modern bar across it to disengage the innocuous lock and let me out. There was, it doesn't hurt to admit it now, even a green illuminated "exit" sign. I pushed the bar. I was outside. Damn it.

To hell with the treadmill.

The next day, back at the round table, we were stuck fast to the ontological and epistemological conundrum that thwarted the discovery of human meaning. After some debate—a transcript of which would read like a slaughterhouse sounds—we fixated upon two central problems, the solving of which would, if not give a proper reason for existence, at least stay the hand of Mr. A, whose frustration at our inadequacy might withdraw the paychecks we each of us secretly knew we didn't deserve and were anyway impatient to receive.

The two problems were thus:

1) sensory inadequacy: that which simply could not be known on account of our limited physical senses not reaching into the real honesty of existence and,

2) captivity: that we are ceaselessly, endlessly, and permanently contained, not free, and any illusions therein only capture us more deeply in the delusion of liberty.

"Imagine it like this," Phil said, "you're a dog."

"I wish there was a zoologist here." (Psych).

"Think," Phil continued, ignoring the quip, "as a dog would. How does a dog see the world? How does it understand existence? What's more salient: imagine what a dog *doesn't* know about existence. That ignorance is analogous to the circumstance we find ourselves in, despite being on two legs."

I wondered if Art had remained on two legs this trip. She and Phy sat next to one another, only pretending to associate with the discourse.

"Or, more appropriately," this from Theo, "the realities of this world are as foreign to us as our world is to a fetus discovering it from utero. If we can imagine the unknown to be as abstract to us as the hospital room and all that comes after is to a baby, than we can begin to recognize how futile it would be to even imagine truth."

"The world that met us upon birth was as thrilling and horrifying as the world waiting to meet us when we transcend," offered Math. My ubiquitous talents of inscription mistakenly attributed, I was charged with taking minutes. I did so longhand in order to miss as much as possible.

"What if," suggested Soc (pronounced long O then *sh*, not like Josh) "when we get to heaven, people are still just as confused? All those answers we expected and the mysteries are still mysterious." He looked over at Theo, perhaps the only non-atheist in the room, to chime in about heaven and all celestial planes. She ignored him.

"It can't all be metaphysics," I said. "Where's our gym teacher?" No one wanted humor.

It boiled down to our need to know; thus, the epistemological problem. Where did knowledge come from and where lay our insatiable need to answer the unanswerable, our appetite no repast could quell? What this made me think of was wondering where Mr. A's motives originated. I wasn't obtuse enough to believe Mr. A was anything but a facilitator, but what did his superiors want from this? What gain? Busi drummed his fingers in rudiment.

Phil looked over and addressed me, "English, isn't there something Walt Whitman says about a kid and grass or something? What is it?" I feigned to be writing the last bit, looked up, didn't answer. I hoped I was giving an inquisitive look (I rubbed my beard for good measure)—I was hungover—my autumns slipping away. I said something about New Criticism and just enough about Derrida to force everyone's ears to mute. Perhaps I was a good professor, after all.

"Art is inherently counter culture," Art said, apropos of nothing but the interests of Phy, whose eyes betrayed a fondness for her heavenly body so much that she could say anything. "It makes culture; to create is to develop culture. And it is a reaction to a previous culture, so it is counter. You cannot be an artist unless you are resisting something." She'd had an exhibit at the Sorbonne, I knew, but I also knew, at her community college, she actually had to *teach* students. Like, teach them Drawing I and freshman Art History and Photo I, where all the boys produced nudes of all the girls too flattered by the lens telling them they were beautiful to keep their clothes on.

"Yes," Phy said, for no reason.

This was how the discourse for problem one went for quite some time. Days. I recorded to the worst of my ability and would transcribe our notes with the jargon of scholarship (where no information ever need be understood nor responsibility taken) for Mr. A.

We also thought long and debated problem two. Captivity.

I don't remember what day it was. Our week was nearing its end. We had been meeting every evening at the same bar. By then, the profs were as cynical as cyanide.

"Freedom is an intrinsic want of mankind," said Psych. He'd been sullen, somber—the expert among us the most outward about his frustration over our processes. In fact, I'm reasonably sure we were all looking at the problem through our own lenses: Psych obsessed with what the exercise said about our cognition; Math trying to organize our ideas in the most concrete terms; Theo spinning in her chair; Soc commenting, "But what about actual imprisonment, as in, mass incarceration?" forcing the rest of us to look at the corners of the room; even me, wondering how our discourse was relevant to the scope of letters—et cetera, ad nauseam. Mors omnibus. So Psych continued, "but freedom is always taken from us."

This was a part of his somberness. He had the teenage pout of an organism evolving just to realize it was better off a legless fish.

"It reminds me," said Phil, "of a story I once read. It was called *A Man Bound*. Kafkaesque. Basically, a man wakes up to find he is in a straitjacket. Once he frees himself, he notices he is in a cage, from which, eventually, he escapes. He then understands himself to be captive in a house which, predictably, he exits. The end of the story has him running around the lawn jumping, presumably frustrated at gravity's insistence that he was stuck fast to Earth."

"And we are trapped in our circumstance," said Phy.

"And trapped by financial insecurities that limit our choices the way bodies limit mobility," said Soc.

"And trapped by those bodies and their decay," said Theo.

"And our countries are traps, a cartographer's mean-spiritedness," said Art.

And Busi—opening a candy, turning with extra effort just to deposit the wrapper on the floor—finally inserted, "We are incarcerated by our lives: we wake, live, and die without knowing why, nor are we able to resist it. We cannot leave the Earth. We cannot deviate from this conscious plane. We are trapped."

"Learned helplessness," retorted Psych.

"Write in your goddamned notes, English," Busi said, "that life's one long, dark hallway that gets colder and thinner the faster you run. And if you have the least intelligence whatsoever, you'll get that straight right away and strive to forget all of the other garbage you've ever learned."

The look we shared could have melted girders.

My hands felt heavy on their arms. I slunk depressed on the way to the bar. This would be my final walk in this direction—days were to be lived in succession, in advance of death. What put me in this mood was the summary I finished just before leaving the hotel and had emailed to Mr. A: the whole reason for existence that was all of our being there (note: I do understand the double-entendre of what I mean: *all of our being there* in the sense of these scholars

149

at this university and *all of our being there* in the sense of humans on this planet). The manuscript, overwrought in twelve-point font, Times New Roman, double-spaced with one-inch margins and footer pagination; concluded exactly nothing. My sorrow wasn't in that we failed Mr. A; to hell with Mr. A. My sorrow was in the nothingness.

Of course, we had methodology; we had summation. We had—all of us through the tint of our different visions—answers, but they were superficial and false and contrived and absolutely nothing. So I did what any good organism trapped in helplessness could to: I went to the bar.

There had developed a sort of nostalgia amongst us, a fidelity to one another betrayed in the discipline pet names, the budding romance between Phy and Art (transecting the middle space between the cellar and attic of the Ivory Tower), the inebriation, and the admission—to a person—of what shams we were. And it wasn't Mr. A's exercise that did it to us; we had known all along. In the dark of the bar with the din insect-to-lamplight buzzing, we were each other's priests because, in finally lacking our pulpits, we could retire to the uniformity and anonymity of the confessional. We would leave the following day, back to our prestige, and so loved deeply that moment of vulnerability where our façade confidences could lower to reveal the scared children we all were, enraptured with ennui, tired to the widest yawn, broken stupid people.

Phy admitted first: "Grad students did most of my research."

My rejoinder: "I know I can't write for shit. I also know it's why my books sell so well."

Theo: "Nietzsche was right."

Soc: "Marx was right."

And so on.

Our professional transgressions aired, we moved promptly to personal insecurities, which of course were the very things we'd regret saying on our respective planes and trains the next morning. Phil explained, "I remember the sad moment when I realized I'd saddled my son with the DNA of my in-laws." Soc rambled without periods or breath: "I was angry at my father for cheating on my mother until I grew up got married and realized adultery is natural—read mid-century American fiction—a wife's sex drive dwindles to nothing and the husband's never diminishes it's only inevitable that this will result in adultery it's not fair that a woman can dictate if they do not want to have sex but the man's needs are ignored he cannot morally choose to have sex with another to satisfy his own needs and so sexual wanderlust equals domestic fidelity: infidelitykeptmefaithful." (Deep breath). Psych joined, "I condemned alcoholism until I started drinking regularly. I'm not an alcoholic but I love drinking; wouldn't give it up for anything. The world is so dire that drinking is necessary." We toasted the notion.

Busi and I had not discussed his final outburst at the round table. He sat, slouched in his pew, sipping away at the foam of his beer, noncommittal (just, in general). Phy came back from the bathroom and sat with the thump a big book makes when shut: vacuum thud. "I liked the notions of the dog and the fetus," he said. Art and he had lost all airs; they held hands above the surface of the table. Maybe something good did come of all of this. He continued, "That was a good way to sum it up. Did that make it into the essay, English."

"Yeah," I said.

"That's good," he responded, and it was.

When it was time to go, we somehow all receded into our belabored atmospheres: we shook hands coldly and rubbed chins and made sounds with our blazers as the pendulums of our arms kept us balanced in our walking away from one another. Our escape was over. Our day-pass dismissed, pardon revoked, parole annulled. We were heading back to the confines of our lives.

Of course, I followed Busi.

Something just wasn't right and I was determined to apprehend him, corner him, cuff him—get answers. I didn't yet have a question but I was sure I'd develop one in the time it took to pursue. I had taken my spirits gingerly that night, knowing I'd make this daring chase, and so was not at all inebriated. I was also not shocked to find us back on campus, back to that door.

I waited; and when I entered, the hallway was lit; or maybe, better, it was lighted. Candles along the corridor had sprung flame and because of it, the entire scene felt cultish, incognito—like Freemasons had bound the masonry, or the Illuminati were a room away in their robes with nude virgins dripping blood. I noticed, on the floor, candy wrappers dropped, not accidentally, but arranged in a line that hinged toward the nearest door and ended in an arrow. Busi knew I was coming.

When I walked in, Mr. A smiled that floodlight smile, "I'm glad you could make it, Pock. Or should I say, English?" He was standing next to Busi in a room unadorned with any furniture. It seemed a supply closet, windowless, but with nothing inside but the two men; I thought instantaneously that they were going to kill me.

"What is this?" I inquired.

"What do you mean?" Mr. A responded. Busi sucked on whatever candy was liberated from the wrapper at his feet.

"I mean," I said, noble, dignified, chin up, "what is this?"

"You already asked that," Mr. A said, "but I don't know what you're asking. This isn't anything."

"It isn't, isn't it? Well what are you two doing here, here, you know, together, right now? What, what's going on?"

Mr. A took a step toward me, noticed my flinch, my boxer's hands aroused and defending, and stepped back, "I'm sorry for the confusion, Pock, but nothing is 'going on.' Our being here right now is no stranger than your being here right now."

I felt had. Got. Preposterous.

"Do you know each other?" I asked.

"We're," Busi answered, "associates."

"Oh yeah?" I countered, noticing more and more how juvenile I sounded, how tee-ball in the big leagues. "Well what does the university think about the two of you in cahoots?"

"The university?" Mr. A responded. "What does it matter what the university thinks?"

He let my pause resonate, then, "Isn't it your employer?"

Mr. A looked at me like a disappointed parent, "And I thought we were gathering the smartest minds of our generation. Truly, Pock, you think I'm employed by this or any college?" Some epiphanies cause numbness. When the light goes on in thought bubbles by our heads, there may come an atrophy; this occurs most when what is revealed only betrays how much is still unknown. Light is what makes shadows. This is watching the magician while he saws *you* in half.

"Then who?"

"It doesn't matter," Mr. A answered. "It doesn't matter who I work for. What matters is that you work for them, too. That this university works for them. What matters is we both got what we wanted out of this transaction."

"The meaning of life?"

He laughed, "Pock, listen to me. I'm sort of an anthologist of ideas. I don't care about meaning, I care about what sells. My employer—*our* employer—has a very vast interest in understanding what and how people buy. The more we know people, the more we know what to sell them. All I did was collect, from you all, the great thinkers, what this might be."

"So," I replied, gaining momentum in my antagonism, "you work for the marketing department of a corporation, is that it? And you used us to better frame your strategy for targeting consumers?"

"Whatever," Mr. A said. "Think about it any way you want. What matters is that you've given us an essay that may assist us this quarter. You got a nice slice. What matters is us, now, Pock. We're what you want *and* what you believe, the money lenders *and* the Temple."

Rage is the appropriate energy.

"And you," I said, nodding at Busi. "You were in on it the whole time."

"Don't act so hurt," Busi said. "This is culture. This is the end game of what we do. You still harbor some delusion of superiority because of your role in academia? You want to know the meaning of life? I'll tell you. Meaning is survival. Any organism that has ever thrived has done one thing: learned the environment in which it lives and made decisions to use the realities of that environment to survive."

"At the expense...?"

"Of everything." A part of him seemed regretful, ashamed: a paralytic stroke part of face, but he wiped it away with the indifference of his kind.

I couldn't respond. What was there to say? I thought of only leaving, forgetting, moving away from this. I turned to Mr. A, "So what do you sell?"

"Everything."

"And our work here was only to help you turn a profit."

"Dr. Pock, we *sell* people what they want and we *tell* people what they want. It's no different than you telling a bunch of students what you think they need to know." I didn't feel like getting into how little I actually taught students. It was over. In our ignorance and ego-centrism they got what they wanted.

Rage is the appropriate energy.

I don't know what Whitman said to the child about grass. I don't know the formula to a great novel. I don't know how to estimate the lifeline of a bar pew in the wood rings, nor how many autumns a man can handle. I do not know the fresh air of freedom. I do not know how wrapper arrows lead us from one thing to the next and why and what for, nor how to confront the soul grinding agony of our Truth. I do not know why we treat each other so poorly.

Consider the dog, the fetus: maybe the mystery *itself* is the freedom we're searching for.

Until we find it: rage is the appropriate energy; overturn their fucking tables.

The Magazine

Their cabin was about as rustic as a middle-class family could tolerate. There was, for instance, plumbing, and even a TV. The log façade recalled an aching past of intemperate seasons along Utah's southern border. Although it was made of real wood, the seams were packed, the walls insulated, the windows double-paned, and the view of Zion's West Temple was unobstructed in the distance save for the occasional flocks of migratory birds. The real estate was precious— particularly to a Nevada family famished by desert and neon—but it cost them years of savings, which resulted in the cabin being relatively small for three. Scott had his own room, but it was no larger than a walk-in closet: a twin bed, a nightstand (lamp), a window; but it didn't bother him. The close walls of the cabin were perfect for closeness, for human contact, for family. Scott negotiated the legs of his parents; his parents negotiated each other. But because, there, they were always on vacation, always hiking and backpacking and hunting and fishing in Kaibab, their contact never warranted anything more treacherous than love.

When it was just Scott and his mother (finally, permanently), she took him to the cabin for the last time. It was winter and the dearth of oil in reserve paralleled the great ferocity of weather outside.

Two years before, when Scott was eight, his father took him to Angel's Landing, in Zion, a mountain peak accessible only by a steep, uncertain hike. The chain rope that marked the trail to the ascent was as high as Scott's shoulders and was the only thing ensuring him against the thousand-foot plummet along the untrustworthy path. He was afraid, an undeveloped fear of heights to describe his then vertigo; but his father insisted he keep going. Scott hated him. But when they finished, surmounted the mountain, and the canyon was wide before him, Scott realized that the hatred he had felt through his fear had become a distinct and profound and unreasonable love for his father. Atop Angel's Landing, it was as if *they* had alighted, spectral, celestial, from a place that could promise perfect peace.

On his stomach, itching against brown shag carpet, Scott bent forward into the crease of the years-old magazine. The scent of the cologne ad was so faint that he had to almost contact the page to access it: the ghost smell of something missing. The cologne ad, like so many of the other ads, was foreign in the way old products harkened to a diminishing past. Dispersed as they were amongst the varying pictorials of animal carcasses and jerky recipes, the ads reminded Scott of something vague, far off, despite the fact that of the ten years of his life, he was only cognizant of the last few. He was fascinated with the magazine: the hunting men, the limp animals, the camouflage. Though still, there was action in the images. A crouched man, bow pulled taut, blue eyes concentrated calmly, with precision, just beyond the camera's focus—perhaps at a deer yards away, equally attentive, for his life.

Another page.

A tree stand. The man it held, rifle ready, glaring out and down, focused unblinkingly (Scott knew, even beyond the fact that it was a photograph, that the man didn't blink) through the browns and greens toward a kill.

He didn't need to read the articles; the photos were enough: captured replicas of the moving world that held their own whole worlds, still, forever. Scott arched his head back to look at the opposite wall; simple, faux wood-paneled, it held only a taxidermied deer head from neck to ten points and a bow, strung but eased limp, upon a nail. Turning back to the magazine, he traced with his finger the striated arms of the men who pulled back the bowstrings, their forearms always roped from the pull, and traced the men's hands around rifle stocks waiting for the command to engage a squeeze, to confirm an explosion. He left his mark there, greasy tokens of identity transferred from finger to page, because everything was uncertain now, in an unclear way he could only assume—fright in the mother's face—meant the end of what they were. A big something suddenly missing.

Scott's mother came out of the bedroom. She was wearing an old bathrobe, frayed at the cuffs and hem, and had the opposite expression than the hunters. Hers was not precision, an obligation to a near object; hers was a flighty absence that seemed to pull her along as if her face were attached to a kite that led her, head then body, forward and up: only where the wind wanted. Scott followed her with his eyes but conspicuously kept his head tilted town toward the pages in front of him, in case she looked. He watched her amble, caught in the clouds, around the small square of the living room, around him, and rest with the hammock-penduluming of a leaf, in the kitchen. From a cabinet near the range she pulled a large pot and began filling it from the sink. Scott watched her, the evaporated scent of the book's cologne not enough to keep him in the pages, the forests. His mother put the pot, now three-quarters filled, onto the stove and turned the flames high.

Strange, he thought, we just ate.

She didn't engage him; she didn't feel the need to explain. She watched the pot and he watched her, an anxiety developing—a thousand-foot drop and his little hand around a couple links of chain. His underdeveloped forearm muscles maybe not roped enough to hold him. *But we just ate.*

And her eyes that stared into the pot.

Scott thought back to their lunch.

She was quiet then, too. He didn't know the word somber, did not (yet) fully understand the emotion of loss, of betrayal; so he did the small things a boy does to demand his mother's attention: foot clapping, humming, dropping clanging things. But nothing.

"Can I have a Coke?" he asked.

She nodded. A small success, a victory, for which Scott would reward himself. He went to the freezer, where they put room temperature cans of Coke to cool faster. The cans, left too long, were often frozen. And something happened where Scott refused his knowledge: he had to thaw the Coke, because his mother's nod was not attention. She was gone, not in the foreign world of pages, but right there, in front of him, somehow gone.

He put the can into the microwave and turned it on.

Scott was no stranger to the basic rules of physics. Nothing long and metal (nothing at all!) into sockets. No electricity near the sink. No metal in the microwave. But doing so was equal to the foot clapping, the dropped clanging; he wanted to reach in and pull his mother, from wherever, back out.

In the microwave, blue lightning danced around the can. Lightning was supposed to be frightening; it was a powerful, destructive thing that struck and disappeared before anyone could give it a proper look. Through the glass door of the box he watched the calmness of the electricity brush gracefully against the aluminum cylinder. It lapped up the side like a dog's tongue; it twisted its fluid branches together, joining longer strands, bending bands that peaked up and split only to reform with blue brilliance on the walls of the box. All of its power left in the grace of its movement; nothing so gentle, so soft, could hurt you.

His mother slapped the stop button. When he looked up at her, she was looking deeply into his eyes, as if he were the animal she coveted to kill.

"Mom?" Scott asked, from the brown shag carpet. He no longer feigned obliviousness; his mother, intent upon the small and slow-to-rise bubbles, wore the look of anger and fear that worked simultaneously to twist a face. She was red behind the developing veil of steam. Her eyes did not blink despite their part in the twisting.

"Mom?" Scott asked again. He could not hide the child in his voice, the smallness of it, weakness. "Are you cooking?" His questions seemed somehow futile, somehow infantile, making him feel so young, when only days before he had promised himself to be older, to stand taller, and not ask foolish, childish questions. He flexed the small muscles of his arms. He had let his mother down by not knowing how to string a bow. How to pull a trigger. How to make a duck call, bear trap, oil change, square knot, wood split, push-up, neck tie, lawn mow, paycheck—make the cologne stay.

She looked at him through the veil and said, "I'm committing suicide."

She picked up the pot of now violently boiling water by its handles and walked directly into the bathroom, shutting the door behind her. Scott watched after. The fire on the stove continued to burn its gas. He watched the bathroom door, watched it not move, watched nothing at all move; even the stove flame stopped—a photograph in which he could see nothing but the lack of movement in things that were supposed to move.

Scott walked back to the center of the common room and back to the magazine, but he could not concentrate on the photographs. The cologne smell was finally, permanently gone. Lightning had struck in the room and it was not blue and dancing. The lightning was how lightning really was. A punch. A swift muscular glossy sweep of force and contact and explosion. Loud. Pain.

Fire.

He tried to focus on the pages but it seemed every image was a carcass. A deer's limp head hanging impossibly from the tailgate of a pickup truck. The green luminescence of a duck's head-feathers hanging lifeless in the awkward grasp of a Labrador's jaws. A bear hunched back against a tree, hanging over the arrow that stuck halfway into its heart. That one commonality: hanging. Of course, the hunters were there too, smiling and investigating, their beard stubble, their camouflage, their carnage; but all Scott could focus on were the animals. What once were animals. The things that remained when the angels left.

He was ashamed not to look, and so he stared.

But Scott was a boy. And his mother was the only thing in the world he felt confident he knew. There would be other things, someday, for sure; but for right then, there was nothing but his mother. Scott got up from the magazine, walked up to the bathroom door, and knocked.

"Come in."

She was naked in the bath, but she had covered herself with a long towel, submerged with her underwater. Saturated, it clung to her body. The pot of water sat on the edge of the bathtub. She leaned over and deeply inhaled the steam still rising from the water. "It clears my sinuses," she said.

Scott looked down at his mother, her skin pruning under the water, her eyes never leaving his face, never betraying for a moment her knowledge that they were fragmented. Family, unstable as off-length table legs, trying to balance even though a whole leg left.

"You're okay?" he asked.

"I'm fine."

Scott turned and left the bathroom. He walked through the common room, onto the brown shag carpet, onto the magazine—tearing the top page—and grabbed the bow before heading outside. Into the woods, but without arrows.

Fellow Elephants

1

As the train speeds up, the things outside become non-things, streaks of things—an angry artist's fist smudge on an abandoned still-life landscape.

Life, too.

I was told as a child, by a great-uncle too deaf to hear any response (too pig-headed to care to), that the slowness that was the time of a child would become the quickness of adult time. That life would soon begin to streak by. I did not understand it then; I understand it now. The hardbound book on the extended table in front of me is titled *Laboratory Notebook* but I know that my father's writing inside is not consistent with any scientific charts or data, and as I fail to affix my gaze on any passing, rushing thing out of the compartment window, my only hope is that the recurring phrase echoing constantly in my head of late is anxiety and not truth: *my poor life is going by.*

I'm taking this train because I miss my father. And going to see him alleviates the adult hurt of missing the once-strong shoulders that can no longer hold me, the masculine love that was as fierce as it was secure. Rough man love like a beard, hurting when rubbed the wrong way but big and sure with razor neglect.

I rest my face against my hand, concocted as it is in the literary-photo way: fist pressed against the mouth with extended index finger out toward the temple for support; and the woman who was unlucky enough to sit next to me commits to the awkward refusal to glance my way. This will end with her neck cramping and my relative ease in the non-dialogic travel. When she entered my compartment earlier, she looked around and attempted small-talk to ice-break by complaining good heartedly that there weren't any TVs on the "darn" train. To which I responded, "I used to scoff at the people in First Class for their privilege over me until I realized I was on an airplane." She'd chewed the sentence but could not swallow, concluding it the traditional non-sequitur of train strangers and, sitting unwillingly, smiled a tranquilizing end to the conversation. I hadn't meant to be short with her but my attention was on the streaking beyond the window and the streaking inside of me and the *Laboratory Notebook* given to me by my father for no discernible reason, but that I cherished.

Dad only ever cried at the thought of a dog dying. Watching films or reading books when a dog was put down, he would (could) weep outwardly, unabashedly, about it, while I watched. I remember once, him reading on a chaise, my mother not at home, and I knew what the text was doing. He was near the back cover, the end of the story, and he began to furrow a telling brow; our family dog, Rusty, lying beside him, while I looked on from the floor. He made no noise, sniffed no snot. But Rusty knew. The pheromones of tears or something. At the paragraph of preparation, the sentence of the syringe, our dog— the real one—got up and went to him, crawled upon him in the way too-heavy dogs believe themselves light-enough, and, beating her tail against his thigh and laying her head on his chest, helped him finish the book. When he was done I went to him and cradled a closed parenthesis opposite the dog, and he held us both while we contained him.

I open the book and try to make sense of the rune-like markings inside that my father had made with his own hand. Some things are clear: the names of students—endless lines of them, a full career of people with whom he'd spent decades in classes. Some names are highlighted. Some have asterisks by them with adjacent notes. There are the obligatory red numbers of grades, the letters of passing or failure at which those numbers converge, and tiny notes of remembrance: "Students threw a pizza party on last day!" and "Jaime wrote her final paper on the 'Yang Tang' theory" accompanied by his sarcastic drawing of a Yin Yang symbol. But there is more in the *Laboratory Notebook* (he never told me why he chose this for his grade book), more than just the cursory markings of a teaching career. Inside, there are human elements—things that speak to the man and teacher he was and that, if read carefully enough, present my father as devoted, spellbound, a man enchanted by that which he chose for himself. Upon his retirement, when he handed me the book, he did so with what I could see as a deep pain. It had been his companion for decades, and closing it etched the permanence of the end of himself as a teacher, which was, in some amount, the end of a part of him as a man. At first, I could not appreciate the profundity of it; but, as is the case, I grew to understand that the value of a text lives deep below its words, so when I finally opened my father's grade book and was able to look past the names and numbers, I saw him.

He'd marked the moment when he'd taught his thousandth

student; the note is highlighted and pen-tip pressed deep, scrawled over again with various colors. I imagined him counting every one until he realized how many students had enrolled in his classes, how many humans he had taught, and knew he noted the accomplishment because he was astonished by it. He'd signed his name to each semester, at the beginning page of each new term, as if to affirm the courses with himself, to authenticate their happening with his presence. His signature changed over the years.

There are whole sections in the back of the book for "pedagogical notes," "memorable semester moments," "extra-curricular service," and "quotes." I romanticize him sharing these quotes with his students:

The great thinkers:

> *There is a time in every man's education when he arrives at the conviction that envy is ignorance; that imitation is suicide; that he must take himself for better, for worse, as his portion; that though the wide universe is full of good, no kernel of nourishing corn can come to him but through his toil bestowed on that plot of ground which is given to him to till.* —Emerson

His own students:

> *There are reasons why Creative Writing is called Creative Writing. The first reason is for the writer to write creatively. The second is for the reader to think creatively.* —Pete Richards

Himself:

> *Slowly, Quietly, Controlled, and Bold.*

I close the book. The woman next to me forces her head forward but I can see the color of her irises as she strains to look sideways at my coded tome. "It's my father's grade book," I tell her, wielding the only fledgling olive branch I can manifest. "He gave it to me when he retired and now I can't seem to go anywhere without it."

"That's sweet," she says, her neck audible in its cracking as she turns to me. "He was a teacher?"

"Yes. I'm going to visit him."

"That's sweet," she says again. "I wish my sons would visit me more."

We let that be what brings us back to silence. Well, almost.

"At least a phone call every once in a while."

I nod my affirmation at parental guilt and progenic

responsibility.

Then it's there. The real silence. And the things outside of the window, rushing.

Dad, do you remember when we were at Fellow Elephants and you told me about your stones? Long before then, there was one of those holidays when the daycares were closed but your school was open, so you brought me with you and had me sit in your office while you taught the Fiction Writing seminar. Contrary to what most parents would have said to their children in their office, you told me to *touch everything*. So for that hour and a half, I took all of the stones from your desk and piled them in various cairns on the office rug. Every stone was differently shaped, differently colored, differently textured, and was clearly of a different substance. When you returned, laden with the joy and exhaustion of teaching, you mustered enough pedagogical energy to tell me the rocks were each from different parts of the world, taken and brought to this singular space. Pointing, you cataloged, knowing I'd never remember: Kilimanjaro, Iceland, Machu Picchu, a Prague sidewalk, Half Dome, Gyeryongsan National Park, Detroit Packard Factory, The Grand Canyon, Cathedral Rock, The Badlands, Glacier…

You went on. And I do remember.

Years later, at Fellow Elephants, I saw you take a rock from the summit of Tusk, after we'd ascended the 5.11c roof crux that you let me lead (I didn't tell you how afraid I was, but you knew and told me it was okay to be afraid). You tossed the rock up and let it fall upon your palm, explaining the moral dilemma of your collecting. *I take rocks like this when I'm in unique and fantastic places. I've robbed mountains and sacred places so I could keep a piece of them with me.* The ones on your office desk, I'd said. *Right. I understand the notion that if everyone did this, the sacred places would no longer exist, and so what I do is wrong, but I take them anyway, mostly because the material memory of the places grounds me.* At work, I'd said. *There, yes. And everywhere. I feel guilty about it. But I also take them so I'll have an excuse to return them. I like the notion, regardless of how false I know it to be, that I'd have to return to these places in order to bring back the stones. Of course, I never have.* Yet, I'd said. *Yet. But I think, because I take from these places, I'm maybe cursed by them. They haunt me for taking a part of them.* I don't think you're cursed, I'd said. I don't think you're haunted, I'd said. *We're always haunted by the things we take with us.*

I flip through the pages of his grade book, thumb at the masking tape desperately holding the spine together, and speak to him as if he's right there. Dad, I have all those stones, too. They haunt *me* now. But in them is you and you are what haunts me but I am not scared.

I was eight when Rusty was diagnosed with cancer of the everything and my father had the duel duties of putting her down and telling me that she had to be put down. I was in that slow time of the child, where doctors could fix anything and fathers (my father) were the strongest people in the world and dogs never died. Maybe it was genetics, or osmosis, but like my father, a dog's death felt to me the most unjust, most desperately sharp wrong of the world. I would lie with her, our parentheses, and stroke the rogue, loose hair from the back of her head while we stared at each other and I felt the ache of love that she was there and the impending anguish of her leaving me. I wanted to just love her as she was there but it kept hitting me like bully punches that she was going to die and I would never see her again. Growing within me was knowledge. At conflict was the childlike sense that nothing bad could happen to me with the new reality that I wasn't as protected from pain as I'd thought.

I lay with Rusty all day. I sopped up her uncontrolled urinating. I kissed her between her eyes and on her cheeks and reveled in her bad breath as she yawned and licked me and occasionally wagged her feeble tail even though.

My dad let me know it was time without saying the worst of it.

Rusty has always been a good girl, you said. *You're going to love her for as long as you live and that is good and that is okay.* You knew that I had to learn something about life that day. You were a teacher and a writer (which is also a teacher) and so every shade of your light illuminated to transmit knowledge, but on the floor there you had no intention of wrenching me away from my dog. You knew that there were things we could not teach each other, that we learn just by experiencing them; so you let me feel it. All of it. *I love her, too*, you said. I'd known that, from the books that made you cry. *And I will miss Rusty with you every day. She's been such a good girl*. Rusty's tail wagged at the old affirmation. *Yeah*, you said, responding to her tail, *you are such a good girl*. And when he spoke to me he didn't do so as a teacher or a father but as a person suffering as much as I was, *It's okay for you to be sad for as long as you want and in any way that you want. But just remember that I'm here. That your mother is here. The thing about being sad when you lose something you love is that it tells you how wonderful it's been to have loved it in the first place.* He wasn't beyond crying, and so did. *Do you want to come?* Of course I didn't but said, yes, I'd come. I didn't want to watch her die, watch the pupils widen when the muscles relaxed, but I wanted to be there for her. When Rusty died, I wanted to hold her, as she'd come to expect me to, so she wouldn't be scared or sad or alone. I told all of this to you, Dad, and I'll never forget what you said, *Can you be there for me, too, Son? I don't know if I can say goodbye to her.* It was that vulnerability, from my most sure anchor, that helped me walk her to the car, to the vet, to the rug in the room, to the needle, to that relaxation, to the point that pulled taut the fabric of our family but because of the family, wouldn't tear it.

The train pulls in to Goshen Junction and my riding partner shuffles to depart; she smiles at me while gathering her things and we exchange the final pleasantries before she goes. Goshen Junction is the halfway point between me and my father. The distance has never been urgent because my father's body and blood is in me wherever I am.

I had a barber once who told me my oddly-shaped head was a result of my parents not turning me when I was a baby. He meant parents should rotate their children in the crib to avoid allowing the soft parts of their skulls to bend in. Dent. Flatten. The insinuation was that I spent a lot of time, in one position, in a crib. That, perhaps, my parent's didn't hold me enough. With scissors so close to my head, I felt it inappropriate to tell him how wrong he was. How much I was held. That my oddly-shaped head was just an oddly-shaped head.

At Goshen Junction I always begin to feel a little anxious. It's not a fear so much as an expectation. I want the train to charge ahead so I can get there faster, so I can see him sooner. My poor life is rushing by. Streaking. But right now the world outside of my compartment window is static, and I can make it out. All of it. I still love Rusty.

In my family, we were all boats, but my father was buoyancy.

2

I bring the book up to the counter and the cashier turns it over a few times before scanning the bar code, "They charge too much for a book like this," she says, goodnaturedly. "You sure you don't want to choose another?"

I chuckle and mock look around the bookstore, presumably taking in the wealth of literature that would be better than that which I am choosing, "Don't worry," I tell her, "I'm not paying full price." She looks back at me in confusion, holding the net result of my brief literary career, brief as a match strike in the wind, in her hand. "Royalties," I add.

She hears this just as she notices the author photo, hand against the face in the traditional literary-photo way; when she looks up, I have that same hand contorted in the same way against the same face. She's quick to correct, "I'm sorry. I…"

"It's fine," I smile, attempting to disarm the embarrassment that will only leave her when I leave the store and board the train that will rush me away. "Me and that guy," I nod at the photo, "aren't friends anymore."

"No really," she lies, "I thought it was quite good."

That *quite*, in all of its archaic placement and inauthentic use, sonar pings its shrill resonance as if leaping itself out of the sentence. "Listen," I say, "if you ever meet an author who is happy with his work a year after it's published, you've met a liar. Don't worry about it. I'm only buying it so someone else doesn't accidentally." My own little lie rests the turbulent look on her face.

"It got pretty good reviews," she says.

"If it wasn't my own creation, my own child, I'd have it burned." At this, she smiles and steps back in order to gain clearance from the counter and retrieve a plastic bag from beneath the register. Her movement is hampered by a late-term pregnancy. She catches me looking. "I'm sorry," I say. I add, to alleviate the intrusion on pregnant women most people feel is acceptable, "Do you know the sex?"

"A girl."

"A girl," I repeat. "Did you know, at this point, your daughter already has all the eggs she'll carry with her though life? In effect, you are also carrying your grandchildren. Well, half of them. You know, the maternal half. Sorry, I'm a teacher so I sometimes teach things without considering if my audience actually wants to be taught."

"No, it's okay," she says. "That's interesting."

My heart rate and circulating blood have been rushing for hours and I am anxious to get home, but I can only go as fast as the train's schedule, so I bide my time. "I've been to two military funerals," I say, a habitual non-sequitur like the ones in my book that one critic called "idiosyncratically quirky" while another called "endlessly gimmicky." "For my grandfathers. They were both in war. After the gun salutes, I walked around collecting the shells to hand out to the congregants." The cashier lays a hand on her daughter and grandchildren. "I guess I have ancestry and progeny on the mind today. I'm going to see my son. Was away at a reading for this," I say, holding up the bag with my book in it.

"Well," she says, "tell him I say hello."

"Indeed I will. Tell her the same when you see her," I say, nodding at her womb. "Good luck," I add, meaning it, as I walk out of the station's bookstore and make my way to the train that will bring me home.

When the train picks up pace it creates a rhythm that is hypnotizing, a maternal heartbeat that can trick you into reverie. Right now, it's as if the cells in my blood are agitated in the best way—they gyrate as they circulate, bounding endlessly in circuit through heart to extremities, backpacking what I breathe. I turn through the first pages of my book, looking for the appropriate blank space for the inscription. Typically, I sign the title page with the obligatory *Best of Luck* or *Thanks for your support* followed by a signature that's changed over the years. But you only get to give your book to your son once, so I search for a larger expanse, finding it only after the hard cover, in the white pasted page glued to hold the book together. It doesn't matter. It's here's I'll write.

Then the delicacy: to be poignant and economic with the words but to exhibit sincerity without feigning the exhibition and to be sentimental without being emotional while saying what needs to be said. You'd think being a writer would help here; but the words seldom come (have ever seldom come) when required. Literature is as random as the beauty of nature; and like it, is far more dependent on the viewer than the artist. I should practice on a napkin first, but I don't.

Son, you should know that (in what seems long ago now but really isn't) in her first trimester with you, your mom and I called you "Little Finch" because we love To Kill a Mockingbird *and I think I wanted to be Atticus. Do know, that I know, that sons don't like sentimental*

fathers, so I'll just say I imagine this book ragged on a bookshelf in your home when you are an old man with children of your own; I imagine you'll go to it, read these lines, and I hope you'll know you were loved.
—Dad

I guess that will have to do. I let the ink dry before I close the book, trying not to reread the inscription for fear that I'll wish to throw the book away and buy another at the next station cigarette stop. My handwriting is big and I wish it was neater; it takes up all the space of the page. I signed my signature. Something about that seems platonic; it's the same signature I use to sign checks. But I suppose it's what you do to books so I did it. Now I get to stare out of the window and wait until I get to see you and your mother.

Being away from home has always been hard, but I suppose when you write a book, they expect you to go talk about it, so I should consider myself fortunate to have an audience, unlike my captive students who never chose me but with whom I'd prefer to talk lit. It's not that I don't like readings, it's just that—okay—I really don't like them. The solitary nature of writing cedes to the public display of the words, where I change hats from being an artist (look at me; I'm calling myself an artist!) to being a businessman, peddling my fare. The word *charlatan* comes to mind, even though, when I'm writing, I feel it's the most sincere thing I do. When I have to sell books, conversely, it feels more ominous—like I'm the Bourgeoisie trying to convince the Proletariat to buy buy buy (remind me to remind you of the problems of graduate school). It feels like what I assume medicine men felt like, touring the countryside to sell pseudo-panacea to gullible idealists. Alright, it doesn't feel exactly like that, but I'm stretching for simile here. At the end of the day, I think I've at least made enough to buy a new dynamic rope and a Grigri. After I figure out how to use it, I'll look forward to teaching you how to use it.

I don't know what makes the rhythm of the train. If I understand the theory of the mechanisms of the machine, that would include metal wheels gliding along metal rails, which should then have a running, constant sound. Perhaps a patient tone that doesn't exactly sound like metal gliding on metal, but buffered by the cars and seats and glass and bodies, the one drone should hum statically on. I don't know what is causing the undulating pulse, but it is mesmerizing. Its hypnosis, and my paradoxical meta-cognitive awareness of being lulled, puts me in mind of all the promises I made about becoming a father. And because I'm somewhat compulsive, I wrote them all down; of course, this may be craft memory—a novelist's tactics of keeping together a woven plot full of dynamic characters (I jest)—but I have a penchant for organization. I don't have the notebook in which I've written down all the paternal promises I made to you, but I don't need it, because I've memorized them.

There may be no merits in illusionary speaking; I am alone in this compartment and am completely silent but act as if I'm speaking directly to you, as if you are here with me on this train being borne back to you and, sitting across from me, you watch my eyes as I say foolish things to a son I desperately want to have understand me but feel as if I am always close to failing. Maybe this is the fear of all fathers. Maybe I feel guilty going to a reading at such a time. I don't know. But it brings me comfort to think of you—perhaps my age— sitting there, looking at my eyes with yours in similar color, listening to me in rapture because I am your father and we are designed—for better or worse—to be enraptured by those who made us. God and papa. But not to ruin the illusion, I will not list the promises I made; sons do not want this of their fathers (they want the promises, they want them, but they do not want them spoken. The silent promise carries more weight than when it is placed upon the faulty mechanism of language). So, I'll tell you a story instead.

Son, once, I was leading on Trunk, at Fellow Elephants, and it was my first time using my own protection. My belayer was a pitch below, connected to an anchor just beyond view; our sightline was obscured by a rock protrusion over which the rope was precariously dragging. The ascent wasn't particularly difficult and the holds were certain but I made the ancient climber's mistake of looking out into the valley behind me and, in positioning myself against its existence, felt my body fall. That is, I imagined the plummet the way vertigo pulls in your stomach, serotonin floods a bunch of synapses, and there's that fraction of a moment where some diabolical Muse tempts you to *just let go*. Despite having my hand deep into a solid jug, I wasn't confident, and felt like I needed to bed down into the bedrock like a deer satisfied enough with the matted grass around him to lie down against any covert jeopardy. I needed security. Near direly, dear diary.

I looked out again and felt the same pang of mortality. This hazard was of my own election; the mountains were there but there was no reason I should go and climb them. If I were to take a fall and my pro sprang from the cracks along the route, I would hit the ground for no other reason than that I was tempted to find the tallest things and make them taller by adding my human length to their apex and make myself taller to see what their peaks see.

At that moment, I closed my eyes and imagined a flutter of used scratch-off tickets on a city street—once hope, now litter. I knew that all things and their worth were a matter of our relationship to them and our consideration of them. When I opened my eyes, I did what was right. I did not think of the valley or my protection or the fall; I thought of the rock that was right in front of me. I focused deeply upon the structure that came in direct contact with my hands and feet. The white chalk-stains of previous climbers who articulated the route with their gripping showed a map of ascent and I hugged my body into the wall, holding the mountain against me. Because it was no longer a mountain. It, at that moment, was nothing more than the surface that was directly in front of me, that which I held. There was no mountain, only a rock in my hands. All that was below and above meant nothing compared to that of where I was. At that point, I lost any concept of what it was to fear.

When I returned home from that trip, I told your mother that I wanted to meet you, and so we began trying to conceive.

Because we wanted to keep you wild, we adopted Rusty.

The train pulls in to Goshen, the midway point. It's here I stand and stretch, thinking back on the previous half of the trip because it acts as a measure by which the rest of the trip will pass. I will only find tranquility when the train starts again, when every moment that passes shortens the second half and brings me across space to meet you.

3

History has far more sovereignty than any one moment's greatest power.

I think this whenever anyone shows too much passion for the politics of the day and also when I consider my father's life. He led a chalk life: at the blackboard and on the mountain, his fingers were always stained ghost-white with chalk dust. At the blackboard, in powder, he wrote vanishing notes that opened new doors for young skeptics; and at the mountain, in powder, he kept his sweaty fingertips dry, to deny the perpetual pull of the same Earth that made the cliffs he loved. History has far more sovereignty, so my father's chalk life is more regal than this moment, when the train begins to pull from Goshen Junction and the things begin to rush again.

Tusk and Trunk were so named for their shapes, as most mountains are. Tusk is a shear big-wall face with high exposure and a sharp ascent that leads to an apex that seems, from the ground, like a singular point. When you get to the top, there's far more space than it betrays, but at the base, it appears you'd have to balance upon one sole at the end of a spit. Trunk, conversely, has a long, arching sweep that makes the first two-thirds of the ascent more of a scramble than a technical climb. You do not need ropes or harnesses or protection; all you need is a little bit of gull, because the ridge you traverse is thin and the plummet on either side is, well, for the falling hiker, the last of things. The last third is a rigid set of pitches with ample protection and clean holds, which makes it a more popular ascent, but it—like its brother—is misleading. Trunk is known to strand a novice climber who comes through a chimney only to find what seems an endless roof traverse with which most want nothing to do. So Trunk demands you drum up a courage you could not have known you had.

Together, the nearby peaks make Fellow Elephants, your favorite place. When I was young, Dad, all you talked about was when I got older, when we would partner up the two summits. As young as three, I remember, we went to nearby crags where you pushed me from my behind to as high as you could reach, while I thought I was climbing by just touching the rock. I got older, and it wasn't long before climbing became ours. My mother could feign joy at the occasional top-rope but could not bring herself to the more precarious multi-pitch routes. So it became you and I who came to know those mountains as intimately as the creases by your eyes when you smiled, or the slits between mine when I'd do the same.

At the top of Tusk, that time you took the rock, you'd asked me, *Do you ever wonder about the selfishness in the notion of wanting eternal paradise?* and looking out beyond Trunk and into the valley beyond, my father butterfly-coiling the rope across his broad shoulders, I had to admit, "No, I haven't wondered about that." But that was only because I was wondering at that present wonder. But now I think eternal paradise isn't so much selfish as it is endlessly elusive, so we can freely want it without the guilt that would come with getting it. I'll make this argument to you when I get there.

Dad, all of the shirts in your closet had their sleeves rolled up, as if you washed them, dried them, hung them, and wore them always with the forearms exposed. I liked thinking that as a metaphor of you getting down to business. As deeply as I can think back, I cannot remember you with long sleeves. If I'd have opened your closet door, at any time, all the shirts would have rolled sleeves.

When I depart from my compartment, a pre-rain mist softens the edges of everything. My father isn't far, so I'm happy to walk the remaining distance. The *Laboratory Notebook*, safe in my satchel, bumbles up and down as I walk, the thousands of names thudding against their grades. At this moment, in the region but perhaps just as likely anywhere, the people with whom those names correspond are moving about the world, climbing their own mountains, or maybe teaching the next thousand. In that way, my father is viral; he believed education was a social, public good, and now spreads outward in the sinews of his students who stretch like the widening fingers of a hand to catch a beautiful hold.

The gates are cold to the touch but do not resist me. Everything is manicured the way it's supposed to be but I can't help but feel something is unnatural about it. The politely cropped grass, the tree branches trimmed to some topiary etiquette, the stones lined by ruler, the solemnity that passes with a coldness not lost upon the nearby chalet of a chapel. We're outside but it's so unlike the wild. I find my father in the perfunctory routine of my feet walking the path of least distance between the gate and his stone. When I'm here, with him, it's as if an elastic band has eased to a resting limpness, but I do not mean to say this as if it were bad or wrong. What I mean is, the tension is gone. Of it. Life. The streaking. Loose, my poor life pauses its going by in the presence of the man who gave it to me and implored me to use it by ascending. I sit cross-legged and withdraw the *Laboratory Notebook*. I have a momentary romantic impulse to leave it at the grave site, like a Jewish pebble, a trace of connection; but it would soon be devoured by rain and happenstance for nothing more than my poetic sentiment, so I just thumb through it, reading the names, reading the notes. *The thing about being sad when you lose something you love is that it tells you how wonderful it's been to have loved it in the first place.* But Dad, that was about a dog. I mean, not to be reductive—our dog—but a dog isn't like a dad. *Sons don't like sentimental fathers.* That *is* something you'd say. I smile at my dad's note, his feigned bravado; even though it was written as the epigraph of the book he gave me, I can hear the tone of his voice in the slant of his handwriting. The tone suggests: I'm trying to hide my sentimentality in case it makes you uncomfortable. But it doesn't, Dad, it doesn't. The last thing you ever made me was uncomfortable. At Tusk, that once (the one once of many), you coiled our rope and stole a stone and had let me lead and asked me if I thought the desire for eternal paradise was selfish. I don't know much about eternity, but I have something in mind for paradise. This condition of ours, to be human, as prosaic as it is, as mean, has its solution in the solvent: when you whittle us away, boil us down, timber our forest—the result is the unthinkable and unknowable attachment that binds us despite the soil between us.

Sitting here at his stone, I feel as tall as I did on Tusk, our stone.

Dad, even when separated, we know each other. Nothing so arbitrary as time, so sovereign as history, could ever nip the elastic. Even now, I can feel the dynamic rope that connects us, as it did on the mountain, here too through the ground.

4

My *Laboratory Notebook* is beginning to fray at the spine and I think to myself two things, unrelated: *fray at the spine* is a phrase I'll have to use one day in a story, and, I need some tape. For the former, this is how my literature comes to me. I almost feel irresponsible for claiming it, for putting my name by a story's title. The words, the words have always been there, hovering in the space around me. I just catch them with a butterfly net and pin them to the page.

The Greeks imagined scantily clad women, Muses, who'd whisper artistry into an otherwise ambivalent ear. For me, creating has been like tripping into a mud puddle and finding silver flakes. A lot of authors liken their work to progeny, thinking their genetic makeup extends beyond them in the texts they shove off into the world, push out of eagles' nests. But these authors aren't fathers, or weren't when they felt this way, or don't think deeply enough about being fathers. Fathering *is* a being. A state of being. It's not a virtue of reproduction so much as a metamorphosis. Chrysalis to butterfly.

I know this now. And with my son, my literature takes new meaning: it can no longer be an extension of me; it is only the silver flake I find after falling. It is with him that I unfurl my unused wings, my crinkled, delicate, and wet new appendages, to ascend.

When there is ten minutes left until I arrive, I begin to get anxious. The final ten minutes of a train ride always near hurt, like how hunger pangs intensify the closer one gets to a kitchen, because the terminus is so near. My hand can reach it faster than this train can glide with its volleying rhythm. My hand, that calloused climbing hand, reaching.

At the station I compose myself so as to not rush from the compartment, out of the building like a madman. The taxis wait at the entrance, so it is no difficulty to hail one and ask for the hospital. When I get there I carry with me only what I brought, into the pupa of my metamorphosis: a satchel and two books. My first published novel and the *Laboratory Notebook* with endless blank pages destined for student names. It was left over from my father's career as a chemist, where in books like this he'd write countless formulae in the predesignated green-gridded squares. Out of graduate school and embarking on teaching (*English!?* he'd said, *Not even a science?* Yeah, Dad, English. He'd smiled, *Okay. English it is. Here take this, for the grades*. It was the notebook) I, of course, had to have something in which to collect my experiences. A diary in red letters and notes. A whole life segregated in semesters.

Your mother is on her back in the room, ready and relieved to see me. I see by her abdomen that I am not late; I can still be the first to meet you. I kneel by her bed and we place our foreheads against one another. She, too, seems different. I can see, without straining, the beauty with which she is prepared to spring, wings extending in unimaginable color.

"How did the reading go?" she asks, incomprehensibly. Even now, she thinks of me, of what I've taken as important. Her beauty extends beyond this metamorphosis; it's always been in her, crawling or flying. I cannot wait for you to meet it. Her beauty and her.

"Fine. People actually bought the dumb thing."

"I didn't doubt it," she says, bravely biting back a wince.

"I forgot to buy puppy food," I say.

"Poor Rusty."

"Yeah, poor dog."

"We'll get some on the way home."

* * *

When we meet you for the first time I realize that for all the
Muses, for all the mud puddles, for all the majesty and sublimity
and incomprehensible divinity of every mountain combined; there is
nothing—*nothing*—words could ever do to record this, so I leave them
fluttering about the air, my net immobile as it should be, on the ground.
And when you hold my finger with what seems a solid clinch, I can't
help but smile and think of rocks. There are, as of yet, no callouses on
your fingers to speak of. But we will make them.

Acknowledgments

A number of these stories have appeared, in slightly altered form, in *The Saint Katherine Review, The Swamp Literary Journal, Kindred Magazine, Glassworks, ellipsis, Apiary, The Evansville Review, The Head and the Hand Press, The Tin Can Review*, and the anthology *Above Water.*

Jeffrey S. Markovitz is a writer and educator living in Philadelphia. His fiction, non-fiction, and poetry have appeared in a number of online and print publications and his books include: *Zero Day Blue Jay* (forthcoming 2025, Tartt First Fiction Award), *The Sharpest End* (2021), US VS (2020), *Permanent for Now* (2018),—*for Olivia* (2013), and *Into the Everything* (2011). He has been nominated for the Pushcart Prize, was published in *The Best Short Stories of Philadelphia*, and was a finalist in the Inkwell Barbaric Yawp contest. He can be reached via his website: www.jeffreysmarkovitz.wordpress.com.